THE
LAST PENDRAGON

John Conlee

Pale Horse Books

ISBN: 978-1-939917-29-4

Cover Design: Sally Stiles

Also by John Conlee:

THE DRAGON STONE

A CUP OF KINDNESS

THE KING OF MUD & GRASS

IN THE SUMMER COUNTRY

THE HEATER

ROUNDING THIRD

THE VOYAGE OF MAELDUN

THE BROTHERS PENDRAGON

CATACLYSM

THE CHAUCER CODEX

Available at: www.PaleHorseBooks.com
Also at Amazon and Barnes & Noble

THE
LAST PENDRAGON

❖ ❖ ❖

John Conlee

Then, in the meantime, there came a damsel that was an earl's daughter; his name was Sanham and her name was Lyonore, a passing fair damsel. And so she came hither for to do homage, as other lords did after that great battle. And King Arthur set his love greatly on her, and so did she upon him. And so the king had ado with her and got upon her a child . . . .

— Sir Thomas Malory, **Le Morte D'Arthur**

Dramatis Personae

Lute — the Earl of Sanham; illegitimate son of King Arthur

Jillian — Lute's wife; mother of Matthew & Editha

Matthew — Lute's son (age 9)

Editha — Lute's daughter (age 6)

Willykin & Eldred — workers at the manor house in Sanham

Old Wat — tenant farmer & grandfather of Simon

Simon — Wat's grandson (age 8)

Tom — reformed thief who became Merlyn's groom (age about 20)

Neely — youth who accompanied Lute from home village when Lute
became Earl of Sanham

Brogan — one of Lute's best men at Sanham & his trusted friend

Mordred — Prince Regent; son of King Arthur & Queen Margause of Lothian;
Lute's half-brother

Sir Colgrevaunce — Round Table Knight; supremely loyal to Mordred

Queen Margause — Mordred's mother; widow of King Lot of Lothian; King
Arthur's half-sister

Sir Agravaine — Round Table knight; son of Queen Margause & King Lot
of Lothian; Mordred's half- brother

Osmond — Mordred's Chamberlain

Magdalene — kitchen worker at castle

Mary — chambermaid at castle; chandler's daughter

Earl Thomas — Lute's uncle; has bequeathed Earldom to Lute

Juliana — Earl Thomas's long-time companion

Gwilym — Earl Thomas's loyal servant

Merlyn — mage; played significant role in the begetting of Arthur and
later of Lute; Nimuë's mentor

Nimuë — Merlyn's precocious female protégé

Raguel — mysterious black stallion with uncanny abilities

Lyonore — Lute's mother

Rob — Lute's boyhood friend

Sir Pelleas — Round Table Knight; capable & loyal to King Arthur

Sir Gawaine — King Arthur's beloved nephew; son of Margause; half-
brother to Mordred

Sir Ewen — King Arthur's nephew; cousin to Sir Gawaine; son of
Margause's sister

Sir Craddock — Round Table Knight; loyal to King Arthur

Sir Sagramour — celebrated Round Table knight; loyal to King Arthur

Sir Kay — Arthur's foster brother; made marshal of castle by King Arthur

Sir Bedivere — venerable Round Table Knight; loyal to King Arthur

Sir Ascomour — fencing master; once taught both Lute & Mordred

Move, Countermove

Chapter 1

The Feast of Michaelmas had come and gone, and the year was on the wane. Still, the early October sun shone down warmly at mid-morning.

Lute had finished re-shingling the eastern side of the barn's roof. Now, pausing to catch his breath and wipe his sweaty brow, he ran his eye over his handiwork. Not bad, he told himself. Should be good enough to see them through several more winters.

It wasn't necessary that he do this job himself—he was, after all, a nobleman, the Earl of Sanham—but Lute had wanted to. Ten years ago, when he had first come back to take charge of the small rural earldom bequeathed to him by his uncle, the ordinary folk hadn't been pleased at his insistence upon doing some of the manual labor himself. But it wasn't long before they grew accustomed to his ways. Indeed, they came to respect him all the more because of it.

"Father!" rang the cry of a young boy from down below. "Father! There's a rider at the gate. He says he must speak with you. He says it's urgent."

Lute looked down over the edge of the high barn. Staring up at him was the animated face of his nine-year-old son, Matthew.

"Father, he's riding a huge black stallion. I've never seen its like."

"Matt, is he an older man with long legs? Or is he a younger man with short legs?"

"His stirrups are high up as mine, Father."

"Sounds like it must be Tom. Matty, run back and tell him I'm on my way."

Lute snatched his shirt and pulled it over his head, covering his strange assortment of chest scars, several which looked like letters that had been carved into his flesh. Now in his late twenties, Lute was strong and fit, and he descended the ladder with the agility of an athlete. He strode quickly across the graveled forecourt of the manorial compound, his young son dashing before him.

At the fortified gateway, Lute saw that the rider and the two guards were chatting amiably. Then the small man on the great black stallion stood up in his stirrups and shouted, "Lute! It's me, Tom!"

"My word," Lute replied. "Look at you, Tom. Goodness sakes, all grown up."

"I'm probably about nineteen, Lute. Probably about as grown *up*" – he raised the hand not holding the reins at shoulder height—"as I'm ever likely to get." Lute recalled that when Merlyn had first taken the stray waif under his wing, Tom hadn't actually known his age. That was more than ten years ago.

The small young man, whose stirrups were indeed about as short as those of a nine-year-old boy, looked completely incongruous on the back of the great black stallion.

"Hello, Rags," Lute said, reaching over the gate and patting the horse on his muscular neck. "You're more beautiful than ever." The horse tossed his head and gave a small snort.

"Ah, still a bit vain, eh Raguel?"

The horse snorted again, and Lute laughed.

"Matt," Lute said, "this wondrous creature you see here is Merlyn's horse. Only three people have ever ridden him."

"And your father, Matthew," Tom said, "is one of the three, 'long with me and old Merlyn."

"*You*, Father?"

"That was a good while ago, Matt, before you were even born. Willikyn," Lute called out to one of the gate guards, "this man's a friend. Let him through."

"Sure will, sir," Willikyn replied. "Thought he might be." Willikyn and Eldred, the other guard, hefted the heavy bar from behind the gate, and then swung it wide open. Raguel, with head held high, danced quickly through.

"You're wise to be takin' every precaution, Lute," Tom said, glancing back at the stout timbers of the gateway. "These be uncertain times we're a-livin' in."

"Breakfast, Tom?"

"I won't say no to that, Lute. . . I mean . . . Sir Earl," he added. He grinned, the title apparently amusing him.

"Matty, run ahead and tell your mother that we have a guest for breakfast. Eldred, would you take the horse to the stables? Wipe him down good and curry him."

"No, no," Tom said, "don't go a-botherin' with that. Hitch 'im to that post over there. I ain't a-gonna be here but just a bit. Only long enough for a quick bite and ta give the earl my message."

Ten minutes later the two men were seated at a table on the covered gallery that ran around three sides of the main block of the manor house.

Matthew and his six-year-old sister, Editha, brought in trays filled with scrambled eggs, hot buttered biscuits, and mugs of cider. Also a bowl of fresh apple slices and a smaller bowl of raspberry jam.

"Editha, ask your mother to come and say hello to Tom."

Jillian, knowing that Tom's unexpected appearance at the manor presaged important matters, had chosen to leave the men to their private conversation. When she came through the door, Tom saw a slightly older, only slightly fuller-figured version of the tall, slender, dark-haired, dark-eyed girl he'd met several years before.

"Tom, this is my wife, Jill."

"An honor, m'lady," Tom said. "I 'member Merlyn and me meetin' you once before. That was maybe ten years ago, back before you 'n' Lute was even married."

"Yes, Tom, I remember that. You were a young boy then, maybe about Matty's age."

"Yes, he was," Lute said, "but not any ordinary young boy."

"Yor right about that," Tom agreed, "I weren't never

no ordinary boy. More's the pity. I'd've traded places in a heartbeat with your young Matthew."

For a moment silence enveloped them. Jill broke it by saying, "Well, I'd best leave you to your talk. It's wonderful to see you again, Tom. I hope it won't be ten years till next time."

"It won't be, m'lady, I can promise you that."

Tom stared seriously at Lute's face for a long silent moment. "Sir," he finally said softly, glancing about to be sure no one else was in earshot, "they're a-comin' for you."

"How soon, Tom?"

"They ain't but a few miles behind me. I followed 'em all the way from the city. This morning I got an early jump on 'em, looped around 'em, and hurried here ta warn you."

"Who is it that's coming?"

"It's Colgrevaunce and a handful of miscreants. Maybe ten in all."

"Coming to do what?"

"Don't think they'll do ya no harm right off. Just want to haul you back to the city. Mordred's been summonin' the nobles from all the shires—and that, o' course includes you—though you are a bit of a special case. That'll be their official reason for wantin' ta fetch you, anyways.

"Lute, you'd best tell 'em yor willin' to go with 'em. But you should insist on takin' along a few of your best men. Cole won't do ya no harm whiles ya be out on the road. Mordred wouldn't want that. But once he's got you back to the city, there's no tellin' what the bastard's got in store for you. I hate ta think on it."

"Will you and Merlyn be there?"

"*Merlyn?* Ya mean you don't know?" Tom's eyebrows shot up. "Lute, no one's seen Merlyn for better part o' three years."

Lute rubbed his chin. He had heard a rumor along those lines, but it had never been confirmed. He hesitated before asking, "Do you think he's dead?"

"Not dead. Definitely not dead. But *gone*. Where, I have no idea. Coulda been a woman that did for him. Old Merlyn always did have a fatal proclivity—word I learned from Merlyn—for a certain kind o' woman."

"Where will you be, Tom? In the city?"

"Rags and I will be around, Lute, but we won't be so visible. Mordred hates us as much as he hates you, if such a thing's possible. You surely ain't forgot what Raguel and I done ta him."

"No, I surely haven't."

"Well, Rags and I had best be on our way. You're likely ta have them visitors within the hour. Wouldn't be such a good thing if they was ta find me here. Not so good for either of us. Anyways, forewarned is forearmed, as Merlyn always says."

Tom gobbled down a final bite of eggs. He snatched up the last few apple slices and shoved them into a pocket—"for Rags," he said. "Thank Jill for me, Lute. I'll know when you get to the city. I'll do my best ta be in touch. If nothing else, I'll leave messages with your Uncle Thomas. Lute, trust no one but the men you take with you." Lute nodded, his lips compressed.

Lute stood leaning against the gallery railing as Tom retrieved the horse from the hitching post and climbed up onto Raguel's back. The horse swung his head toward Lute and gave a loud whinny. It seemed to Lute that a bright light gleamed from the black stallion's large amber eye—straight at him.

Lute was still leaning against the railing five minutes later, looking pensive, when Jill came and stood next to him. She put her arm about his waist.

"It seems I'm being summoned to the city, Jill," he said.

"I suspected as much."

"I shall miss you and the children."

Jill squeezed her arm more tightly about him. "We shall miss you, my husband. We shall miss you very, very much."

Chapter 2

To Lute, Uther Pendragon's great city looked much as it had when he'd first laid eyes on it over a decade ago. He'd stopped at just about this very spot on the crest of this same high hill. There, across the intervening valley, the city rose up in its several imposing tiers; and there, crowning the top of the highest tier, was the many-towered citadel. Lute ran his eyes around the high, gleaming white walls that enclosed the whole city. And there, along the entire left side, blue in the bright sunlight, flowed the broad river that formed a natural moat around two-thirds of the city. Lute looked across at the high wooden bridge that spanned the river in front of a massive, two-towered gateway.

He remembered how amazed he'd been at his first sight of the city, and how excited. Right at that moment, he'd felt sure it was where his future lay. He'd been right—more or less.

"Holy Jerusalem!" gasped a voice close beside him. It was Neely's voice. Like Lute back then, Neely was now seeing Uther Pendragon's great city for the first time. "It's wonderful!' he declared.

"Yes, Neely, it's like nothing else in the world—except

maybe that holy Jerusalem you just mentioned." Lute smiled at the lad on the horse beside him. "As I once heard Merlyn say, 'Uther Pendragon, for all his faults, was good at some things. Designing his magnificent city was one of them.' But Neely, a place, in and of itself, is neither wonderful nor terrible. It's the people in it that make it what it is."

Neely paid little heed to Lute's words. He stared in awe at the sight. "Lute, does that river flow down to the sea?"

"Yes. Do you see that little glint of light way off to the west?"

"I do, I do."

"That *is* the sea. Do you see over there," Lute said, pointing, "where the river flows into the broad estuary?"

"I do, Lute, I do."

"Now follow it with your eye. In a mile or two, it reaches the sea."

"Yes, I see it now!" Neely studied the entire panorama. "Oh, Lute," he suddenly declared, "them little specks over there, them's people!" Neely had spotted the narrow roadway that wound up through the water meadows toward the bridge and the city. "Them's people and wagons!"

"And horses, oxen, and mules," said a deeper voice. It was Brogan's voice, the other companion who'd been allowed to come with them from the manor. Lute had initially requested permission to bring four men. Colgrevaunce had insisted on his bringing just one. Finally they'd settled on two. Lute had chosen Brogan because he was one of his best laborers, and though a man of only modest intelligence, he was a powerful physical specimen with unlimited energy. In a scrap, he was the kind of man you'd want to have at your back.

Neely, in contrast to Brogan, was just a wide-eyed youth. Small and slight of build, he was quick of hand and foot, reasonably bright, and he had an inexhaustible supply of optimism. Neely was the one person Lute had brought with him to Sanham from the remote hamlet where Lute had grown up, the tiny village called Northering, where Lute's mother still lived. Lute had known Neely for the whole of the lad's life. From the time he was three or four, Neely had idolized Lute. His loyalty to Lute was absolute. And now, his innocent delight at seeing the city was typical.

"Well, Sir Earl," sounded Colgrevaunce's voice, tinged with scorn, "here we are. I hope you'll be as pleased to see Mordred as he will be to see you." Then he laughed.

"I can hardly wait," Lute replied. "Do you think he's prepared the fatted calf?"

"Ha!" came Cole's response. "Well, let's go, men," he called out. "There's a tavern over there where I believe they know my name."

"Maybe there's two or three of 'em," one of his men said, and the others laughed. So did Colgrevaunce.

The little cavalcade set off, journey's end half an hour away.

❖

Just below the top of the highest tower in the citadel's central keep, a solitary figure stood looking out across the wide valley toward the ridge of hills from which Colgrevaunce and the other riders now descended. Mordred often came here to be alone. He loved to look down upon this great city—once Uther Pendragon's city, once Mordred's father's city, and now *his*. Or so Mordred wished to believe.

Sometimes when he was alone like this, Mordred's mind entered a peculiar kind of reverie, almost a waking trance. Today it didn't. Instead, he found himself reflecting on his plans for the coming days: his impending coronation; his impending marriage to the queen; and the adulation he expected to receive from nobles and commoners alike.

But as much as any of those things, he looked forward to the final humiliation of Lute, his half-brother, who was just a few months his elder. Exactly what shape that humiliation would take, Mordred didn't know. He hadn't decided on it yet. A public execution? Definitely not. It would be something much more personal and private, something that involved just the two of them.

Thinking of the queen, he glanced off to the left toward the separate but connected royal dwelling, a smaller edifice within the larger complex of structures in the citadel, an impressive building that was more palace than castle. That's where the queen's chambers were, and right now, Mordred hoped, she was involved in whatever preparations she needed to make for their wedding.

Closer to where he now stood were the lavish

apartments of Mordred's mother, the Queen of Lothian and one of his most trusted advisors and confidant. Margause was the one who'd orchestrated many of her son's nefarious actions; and it was because of the talisman, an inscribed ring, she'd given him years before, that he'd manage to survive several near fatal experiences. At least, that's what both of them believed. To her son's consternation, Margause was now opposed to his marrying the queen. But for once, he had no intention of heeding her advice.

For a moment a dark cloud scudded across the sky from the west, briefly occluding the sun. Dark shadows fell suddenly on the city. Involuntarily, Mordred shivered. He pulled his cloak about him and waited for the cloud to pass on its way.

An hour later, Mordred entered his mother's private chambers in the castle. She was seated in a cushioned chair near a window that looked out upon the castle gardens.

Mordred paused for a moment to look at this lovely woman with lustrous, deep-red hair. She still looked youthful though she was well into middle age. He knew that, to most men, she was still a very desirable woman. Of course *he* didn't desire her, did he? Though he could understand her arousing such feelings in other men—as a younger version of her had once done in his own father.

"You fool!" Margause spat at him suddenly. "You're having him brought *here?* You should have had him killed years ago. Why here, why now?"

Taken aback by her unanticipated outburst, Mordred had a moment of fright before collecting himself.

"Mother, I'm bringing him here because I want him to be present at my coronation. I want him to see with his own eyes what he will never have. And then, Mother, I want the pleasure of dispatching him myself, in my own way, with my very own hands."

"Mordred, your vanity will be your undoing. There is great danger in having him here. There is great danger in his still being alive."

"I know that, mother. I like that. I like the great danger. It gives spice to life."

"Well," she replied, "I know a little about *that*," a smirk upon her lips. "The very act through which you came into being had a great deal of danger, and oh yes, a great deal of spice. But Mordred, now that we've nearly reached our goal, caution and clear-thinking are called for, not danger and spice.

"And what of the queen? Do you really intend to proceed with your ridiculous idea of marrying her?"

"I do."

"Madness."

"Why? You know she never really loved him," he said. "Nor did he ever really love her."

"Mordred, it's *incest!* In the eyes of the Church, man and wife are one flesh. Marrying your father's wife, even if she isn't your mother, is *incest*."

"Then that will bring matters full circle, won't it, Mother? A pleasing symmetry." Mordred was referring to his own begetting, the result of his father's union with his own half-sister.

"Mordred, it will make you doubly damned."

"Well, as long as I am the king, I couldn't care less."

"The people won't like it, Mordred."

"I think they will, Mother. The people love their queen. They will be glad that they still have her as their queen."

Margause sighed. "Mordred, you are forgetting one thing. It still hasn't been proved that the King is dead. What if he *isn't?* What if he comes back?"

"He won't. But if by some miracle he is still alive, which seems unlikely, then we shall have to make certain that he never comes back."

"You seem very certain of a lot of things, my son. Maybe *too* certain. Perhaps having, or at least pretending to have, just a little humility might be more becoming."

"Humility?" Mordred said, smiling. "I must learn the meaning of the word. Maybe Lute can teach me."

"Mordred, . . . get *rid* of him. There is great danger in his still being alive."

Chapter 3

Sir Colgrevaunce and his little band led Lute and his companions through the lower levels of the city and on up to the highest tier where they entered the great citadel itself. There would be no comfortable lodging house for them on the city's third tier, the next to highest level, the one where most of the lesser nobles in the city lived, as did Lute's Uncle Thomas. Lute suspected they were going to be housed in more meager quarters and held under lock and key as noble prisoners. Lute didn't say anything to his two companions. Neely glanced about him nervously, Brogan looked impassive.

Their horses were led away to the castle stables, and the three men found themselves being shunted up steep steps into the central keep. As the little group progressed, many people in the castle paused to eye them, curious as to who they were and what was going to happen to them. One man in particular caught Lute's eye, a tall, hawk-faced, ginger-haired fellow who seemed especially interested in them. Lute felt sure he'd seen the man before, but couldn't remember who he was.

Now he had it—the man was Sir Agravaine, one of the king's nephews and Mordred's half-brother. Lute had only seen him a few times long ago, at a couple of the great royal feasts, though he knew the man by reputation. Of his four brothers, so he'd heard, it was only with Agravaine that Mordred had formed a close bond—the other three preferring to have as little to do as possible with Mordred, their inscrutable youngest brother. And now, as Lute recollected, of the five brothers, it was only Agravaine who remained alive in the city. Sir Gareth and Sir Gaheris had met tragic deaths in a chaotic misadventure, an event that had also resulted in the deaths of many other knights and the destruction of the Round Table fellowship itself.

It was following the deaths of Gareth and Gaheris, Lute knew, that Sir Gawaine had persuaded the King to cross the water on what turned out to be a disastrous, misguided attempt to wreak vengeance on Sir Launcelot. It was still unknown whether either of them were alive, the King or his beloved nephew.

As for Agravaine, he stood and watched as Lute and his two companions proceeded on up the stairway. He knew where they were being taken—to a small, private chamber high up in the western-most section of the keep. Agravaine hadn't known Lute during that brief period when Lute had been in the city training for knighthood. He wouldn't have been able to put a name to the fellow now, except for the fact that he was fully aware of his brother's keen interest in him. Agravaine and Mordred shared many confidences, Mordred's intense hatred for

Lute being one of them. Agravaine knew that his brother had special plans for this man. He didn't know what they were, but he knew that whatever they were, the consequences wouldn't be pleasant for Lute. Agravaine couldn't keep himself from smiling at the thought.

In the small apartment to which Lute and his companions were led were two rooms. The larger one, which was none too large, was for Lute; the smaller one, an antechamber really, would be shared by his men. The rooms were simply appointed. They contained low, narrow beds with straw-filled paillasses; a wooden table in Lute's room, none in the other; three-legged stools in both rooms; and chamber pots. Each room had a small fireplace, but there was no sign of kindling or fire logs. Each room had a small casement window, Lute's being slightly the larger. Lute's window had both an external and an internal wooden shutter and an iron hook to secure them together. The windows provided the only light.

Lute dropped his knapsack at the foot of his bed and stepped over to his window. He leaned out and looked down. Below him, a good one hundred and fifty feet, was a small inner, flag-stoned courtyard. Across from his window he looked upon the blank, windowless wall of one side of the massive central keep, the stones appearing cold and gray. By craning his neck and looking up, Lute could just see the elegant outline of the citadel's highest tower. Atop it, on a tall staff, flew Uther's Pendragon's famous banner displaying a red dragon on a field of green.

Lute turned his eyes back to the small, bare, fireless room. He knew that it was little more than a prison cell. At least they hadn't been deposited down in the murky depths of the donjon.

After they'd stepped into their new abode, they heard the stout oaken door close behind them and a bolt on the outside slide into place. Through the door they could just barely hear the voices of the two guards posted there. Lute and his companions were now entirely at Mordred's mercy.

Two hours later there was a tap at the door. The door was unbolted and opened, and a pair of women entered the anteroom carrying wooden trays. They'd brought the men a slender meal of bread, cheese, and small beer. The women moved through the open door into Lute's room and placed the trays on the table there.

"Thanks, Miss," Brogan said in his guttural growl. The women eyed the trio of men with obvious curiosity, and the taller of them gave Brogan a shy smile. Neither of them spoke. They turned about and departed.

After half an hour they came back to collect the trays. Another man entered behind them. "Sir," the man said, politely addressing Lute, "in an hour I shall come for you. Please be ready." Lute nodded. He wasn't sure what he was expected to do to be "ready," though he guessed he was about to have an audience with Mordred. He wasn't wrong.

An hour later Lute, accompanied by a trio of guards, was

hurried along dark corridors dimly illuminated by rush-lights in wall sconces. Mordred's spacious chambers, Lute soon discovered, were located on the opposite side of the great keep, on about the same level as the rooms where Lute and his companions were sequestered. As they neared those chambers, the splendor of the archways and doorways increased in architectural sophistication and ornamentation. Obviously, they had now moved into the royal portion of the keep.

The guardsman's knock was answered by an emaciated-looking fellow in a plum-colored livery. He gave Lute a squinty-eyed look, then gestured with his head for Lute to enter. The door snapped shut. Without speaking, the man ushered Lute into a larger room. The furnishings, the tapestries, the carpets were all of the finest quality. Lute gave an inward smile at the contrast between this room and the one he'd been given.

There, seated by the window with his back to them, was a man dressed mostly in black. At his elbow stood a goblet and a carafe of red wine.

"Sire?" the man with Lute said, finally speaking. "He's here."

The man by the window took his time turning about in his seat. Then he slowly raised his face to look at Lute. "Why, so he is," he said. He paused for a long moment before saying, "You may go, Osmond. Close my chamber door after you, if you'd be so kind." The man did so.

"Well, *Brother*," Mordred said, "sit, sit." He motioned Lute toward a chair across from him. He didn't offer him any wine. "When last I saw you," he said, "how many years ago was that?—you'd just reamed me through the middle, reamed me with my very own precious sword. Do you remember all of that? Or have you forgotten?"

Lute hesitated a moment before saying, "Yes . . . I do remember . . . though I was barely conscious myself."

"Dear Brother, I initially thought that I'd killed you. And then you thought that you had killed *me*. And the joke is, we were both wrong!" Mordred smiled, but it almost looked like a grimace of pain.

"I did think you were dead, Mordred," Lute said. "Though as I remember it, it was you who'd pretty much impaled yourself on the sword that I had grasped."

"Yes, perhaps you are right. Though you did give the sword a pretty good extra push, as I recall. Anyway, it's all water under the bridge, as they say. Maybe we should show each other our scars, compare them, for old-time's sake? I'm guessing you have a few more than I do."

"I have a good few," Lute replied. "Many of them your handiwork, though not all. Probably about half."

"Ha, ha. All I have are the ones you gave me, aside from a couple of smaller ones on my forearms contributed by Sir Lamorak. That pig-headed fellow just wouldn't concede defeat; he insisted upon going down fighting."

"Sir Lamorak is dead?" Lute asked.

"Oh, indeed he is. You don't know much, do you, Lute—living out there like a bumpkin in your little country earldom, so far away from where all the important events of the world are occurring. For the life of me, I can't understand why you chose that. Goodness sakes, Lute, you and I could have been vying with each other for the rulership of the kingdom. That would have been wonderful fun. But you went and denied me all that pleasure by disappearing into the hinterlands, choosing to live like some peasant farmer—or so I've been told. Shame on you, Lute. Uther Pendragon's noble blood flows through your veins. You are no farmer. You were meant for more glorious things. When my men came for you, you were probably doing something menial like shingling the roof of a barn." Lute gave a tight-lipped smile but said nothing.

"Actually, that wasn't just a guess. My men told me."

"Simple pleasures, Mordred. I don't think you would understand."

"You are right about that. But Lute, let's get down to business. I've summoned you here because I want you, since you are my brother, to play a major role in my coronation—do you think you could do that?"

"I doubt that you intend to let the world know that I *am* your brother."

"Goodness no, I certainly couldn't do that. But I don't mind letting the world wonder about this strange, unknown fellow who's suddenly playing an important part in the festivities. Lute, it will add spice to them."

"What role did you have in mind?"

"So you'll do it? Splendid," Mordred said. "We will have to get you fitted out in some clothing suitable to your noble station."

"What role did you have in mind, Mordred?" Lute asked a second time.

"How about this? After the others have bestowed upon me the robe, the scepter, and the orb, and after my head has been anointed, why don't *you* be the one to place the crown upon it?"

Lute was speechless at the ludicrousness of what Mordred had just described. But Mordred's idea of having Lute publicly endorse his kingship hadn't escaped him. That would tell all and sundry that Lute had renounced any claim to the throne—if the matter ever arose, which it wouldn't.

Mordred, seeing the wheels turning inside Lute's brain, grinned at his half-brother.

"You like?" he said. "You, Lute, would be right in the center of things. You would almost be the man of the hour. Almost, but not quite."

Just at that moment they were interrupted by a loud thumping on the outer chamber door. Seconds later, a man burst into Mordred's private chamber. It was Sir Agravaine. "Forgive me sire, but I have urgent tidings."

"What is it, my brother?"

Agravaine hesitated, glancing at Lute.

"Anything you say can be said in the presence of this man," Mordred said. "He is one of my most trustworthy noblemen, the Earl of Sanham. We were just discussing the role he might play in my coronation."

Agravaine hesitated a moment longer, shrugged, and then said, "Sire, it's the queen."

"The queen? What about the queen?"

"Sire . . . she's gone."

"*Gone?*"

"Apparently she's fled to London, sire. Sir Kay and Sir Bedivere have absconded with her."

"*Merde!*" Mordred shouted. He threw his half-filled wine goblet across the room, leaving a trail of bright red on the carpet. "And I trusted her! I *trusted* her! Oh, my brother, Kay and Bedivere shall pay dearly for this. Oh yes, they shall!"

CHAPTER 4

Sounds made by the swiftly flowing river filled the air. Merlyn looked out from the small, cave-like chamber, high up in the Wye Valley, a chamber he himself had helped to carve into the hillside. Merlyn was here in his special place, a place to which he'd always retreated when in need, a place he always considered home. Now, ironically, it was likely to be his home permanently.

Why had he thought it was safe to bring her here? He should have known better. But, as they say, there's no fool like an old fool. He grimaced. She had been so eager to learn, and he had been delighted to teach her. She had been the perfect pupil in every way. And yet . . . and yet.

There was no visible, physical impediment to his leaving the cave. But though the "wall" that hemmed him in didn't seem to be there, it most definitely *was* there. How had she learned that spell? He didn't actually teach it to her, did he? Well, he must've done.

But what had she been afraid of? Of course, he knew the answer to that, too. But Merlyn still tried to convince himself he'd had no evil designs on her. He hadn't, had he? But the truth was, she had known better what was in the old man's mind than he had. Merlyn sighed. He stared out through the opening of the cave and its invisible barrier. He listened to the sounds made by the leaping, tumbling waters of the River Wye.

❖

"Lady Jillian?" Willikyn called in a loud voice.

Jillian stepped through the door of the manor house and out onto the covered gallery. "Yes, Willikyn, what is it?"

"My lady, old Wat is at the gate. Says he wishes to speak with you. Says it's important."

"Let him in, Willikyn, and send him right up."

Jillian stood by the gallery railing and watched as Willikyn hurried back down to the main gateway. Only a few moments later she watched as the old man strode up across the open courtyard. She knew he was quite elderly, yet it pleased her to see how confidently he moved. Old Wat had long been one of Lute's favorite tenant farmers, and once the two of them had stood together in an event that contributed significantly to the history of the little earldom. Together, along with a few sturdy farmhands, they had taken down that vile fellow, Oswald, who'd abused his position of trust as interim overseer of the manorial estates. That was ten years earlier, an event that restored control of the earldom to Lute's uncle.

Now the old man stood looking up at Jillian. When he whipped off his cap and held it in his hands before him, his sparse gray hair sprang out in all directions. Jillian suppressed a smile.

"My lady," the old man said, with a dip of his head.

"Walter, won't you come up and sit? It's a pleasure to see you."

"My lady, I believe I will. Got a few things ta tell you, if'n you'll lend an old feller your ear for a bit."

"Of course, Walter, please come up."

Wat climbed the set of steps located at the nearest corner of the central manor house and stepped quickly along the gallery to where Jillian was now seated. She motioned for him to take the chair opposite her.

"Would you like something to drink?" she asked.

"Oh, naw, naw, but I do thank thee all the same. My lady—"

"Please call me Jill, Walter."

"Well, all right, so long's you call me Wat."

"It's a deal . . . Wat," she replied.

"Jill. I'm a-wantin' ta ask a favor." He paused.

"Go ahead, Wat, I'm listening."

"Your boy, Matthew." He paused again.

"Yes, what about him?"

"Well, m'lady, Simon, my grandson, who's about Matthew's age, is a-comin' ta stay with me for a bit. And I was a-wonderin' if your Matthew could come too. The two lads could help ta occupy each other, don't ya know, makin' it a bit easier on my old bones."

"Of course, Wat. When he's not at his studies or chores. I think he could come to your farm daily."

"No, ma'am, that's not what I'm a-meanin'. My lady, I'd like him to come and stay with me for a bit."

Jill was taken aback. What did he mean by saying he wanted Matthew to do more than just *visit* the farm? Why would he want him to come and stay?

"Walter, I don't understand."

"M'lady," Wat said after a long moment's pause, "there's something I think neither you nor Lute have thought about."

"And what would that be, Walter?" she said, forgetting for a moment to call him Wat.

"Jill, I'm a-guessin' you know who Lute really is. You do, don't you?" Again, Jill was momentarily stunned by the old man's question.

"Well . . . yes," she finally replied, " . . . I guess I do. But neither of us think about that very much. That's all ancient history."

"Beggin' your pardon, m'Lady, but it ain't. Not now that Mordred's summoned Lute to the city." Involuntarily, Jillian shuddered. Then, reluctantly, she nodded.

"M'lady, Lute's in a direct bloodline to Uther Pendragon. And that means Matthew is, too. M'lady, the lad must be gotten out of harm's way. After that bastard Mordred has done whatever he plans ta do with Lute—and I don't like thinkin' about that—Matthew's likely to be next, once the bastard, beggin' yor pardon, brings it to mind."

Jillian twisted her hands nervously before her. Such matters hadn't even crossed her mind. Now they did.

"Let me take the boy for a bit. The two boys can do their lessons together. And I'd love to teach Matthew woodcraft, just the way I did Lute's Uncle Thomas."

The two of them sat there in silence for a full minute.

Finally Jillian said, "Okay, Walter, we shall try it. But I do have one request."

"What would that be, m'lady."

"In addition to wood*craft*, you teach Matthew the art of wood*carving*."

"Woodcarving?" the old man said, grinning. "Well, yes, I do know a bit about that."

"I know you do. I've seen your work."

"What work would that be, ma'am?"

"A lovely wooden bowl with the twelve signs of the zodiac carved around the rim, each one with an amusing, cleverly carved face."

"Ha, ha. My long-ago gift to Lute's mother. I 'member a-makin' that bowl."

"Lyonore greatly treasures it, Wat, and Lute was always quite fond of it, too. He loved showing it to me. He did it on several occasions."

"M'lady, I wonder if these old fingers o' mine can still do sumpthin' like that. I'd love ta do sumpthin' similar for you, m'lady."

"Walter, when will you be wanting the boy?"

"Soon's possible, my lady. Simon should be arriving Friday."

"I'm sure Matthew will be pleased. He's been at loose ends since Lute departed for the city. Misses his father terribly—as do I."

❖

Tom slipped in among the motley assortment of folks hurrying through the city gates. He looked indistinguishable from several other young teenagers returning from their day's hard labors in the fields. The warning tolling of the curfew bell had sounded only moments before, and the gates were about to be shut for the night.

Tom was on foot. He had left Raguel about half a mile away at the cottage of a tenant-farmer friend—the beast far too magnificent to go unnoticed in the city, and there was no good place there for Tom to keep him.

Darkness fell swiftly on this early October evening, and once the shadowy group of stragglers had cleared the great gateway, they dispersed quickly in various directions. Tom glanced up at the raised inner portcullis as he passed beneath it, then stepped up his pace as he entered the large market square on the lowest level of the city. He skirted the central fountain and hurried toward a small chandler's shop. He hoped the chandler's daughter, who was his special friend, would be awaiting him. Tom knew that Mary began her days early, climbing up to the castle where she was a chambermaid, but that she was normally home again by early evening.

As Tom slipped silently through the back door of the chandler's shop, his nose was greeted by the smell of freshly baked bread.

"Oh, Tom, you're here!" came the girl's whispery voice.

"Aye, Mary, it be me. But I do be a bit fagged out."

The young woman embraced him, then pulled a stool out from beneath the kitchen table. Tom plopped down on it. Mary poured ale from a large, earthen jug into a wooden goblet and handed it to him.

"You're an angel, Mary." Tom drank deeply from the goblet.

She removed a loaf of bread from the warming box and sliced off a thick slab. She lay out a wooden plate for the bread and set down a pat of butter and a small bowl of jam.

"There's cheese, if'n you want it."

"This be grand, Mary, grand," he said, smiling at her.

The plumpish young woman, with rosy cheeks and light brown hair tied back by a scarf, had just turned sixteen. She and Tom had been courting for several months now, and they were comfortable in each other's presence. They'd first met when he'd worked as a hostler in the royal stables in the castle, she as a chambermaid. Tom had always had a special knack for horses. He was happy working there until the day Mordred caught a glimpse of him and recognized him as the young fellow who'd played a key role in his near demise. Tom, realizing that Mordred had recognized him, didn't wait about. He was away from his job in a flash. But, although there was now danger for him to be in the city, he'd continued seeing Mary surreptitiously. They'd kept their relationship under wraps, except for her father, who didn't object. Her father was also fond of the lively young fellow, who sometimes lent him a hand in the candle making.

"Tom, I was so worried," Mary said. "The city is a-buzz with rumors and gossip. I was afraid some of it might involve you in some way."

"Not just yet, Mary, but give me a chance. Perhaps it still will."

"Oh, Tom, don't be a tease."

"Me, a tease? Well, maybe just a bit of one. But Mary, in all seriousness, I need to pick your brain."

"There's not a lot to pick, Tom."

"Oh, indeed there is. You, my dear girl, are a fount of knowledge. I need to drink from that fount."

Over the next hour, Tom quizzed Mary, tapping into her knowledge of the castle's many chambers and passageways. By the time their conversation was over, he felt he had a very good notion about where Lute and his companions might have been stashed away. Tom already had some first-hand knowledge of the castle, but he'd never set foot in any of the upper portions of the complex structure.

Mary came and stood behind Tom. She draped herself over his back and shoulders, her head against his, and ran her hands gently over his chest.

"You're a peach of a girl," Tom said. 'You have it in you to save this city from a terrible destruction. Did you know that?"

"No, Tom, never me. But I don't doubt that you do, my love."

❖

Merlyn hadn't had the recurring dream—a nightmare, really—in several years. Not until last night. It had usually involved the city being engulfed in a totally destructive conflagration. This time it was an earthquake, with foundations cracking, buildings collapsing, fissures opening in the city squares, the high defensive walls tumbling in, people running, screaming, crushed by falling masonry, dying.

What did it all mean? Was it a prophetic dream? Or an allegorical vision of some kind? Whatever it might mean, given his current circumstances, Merlyn wasn't in a position to do much about it. Merlyn thought about Macrobius's six types of dreams. He felt sure of one thing: his dream had *not* been the result of indigestion—it had been days since he'd eaten much of anything. Was it caused by starvation?

Suddenly the figure of Tom came into Merlyn's mind. That happened sometimes, which usually meant his young protégé was up to no good. Merlyn wondered what it might be this time. Then it was Lute who entered Merlyn's mind—Lute, on whom he'd pinned such high hopes; Lute, who had stayed true to his own simple values and modest desires, desires that had surprised even Merlyn. And then into Merlyn's mind came Arthur, Lute's father, a man Merlyn loved as much as Lute. Where was Arthur now? Would he ever return? Oh, my, there was so much Merlyn didn't know.

Finally, intruding sharply into Merlyn's mind came

the image of the great black stallion. The creature seemed agitated. What could he be fretting about? Did the sudden appearance of Raguel's image mean that the horse was thinking of Merlyn? Could it mean that he was coming to him? Yes, Merlyn decided, that must be it, the horse was planning to come. But why? Was there something urgent the horse needed him to know?

Who, or what, Merlyn wondered for the thousandth time, *was* that remarkable beast? Was he some kind of projection of Merlyn himself? Perhaps. Whatever he was, Merlyn, despite himself, had come to love that great black stallion. He found himself missing the horse mightily. He hoped Raguel was coming. He longed to see that beautiful, enigmatic creature.

Chapter 5

Lute, Brogan, and Neely were in Lute's larger room, chess pieces laid out on the low table, a game in progress. Lute, quite an expert player, had been teaching the game to Neely for several months back in Sanham, and the youth had caught on quickly. For Brogan, chess held no interest at all. At the moment, Lute was pondering the board intently, for Neely had pinned his queen with a combination of rook and knight. It looked like Neely might actually win a game from Lute, something he hadn't yet done.

While Lute considered his next move, Neely stood and walked over to Lute's window and looked out. He stuck his head through the opening and peered down at the flagstones of the small inner courtyard far beneath them. He shuddered. "That is a long way down," he muttered nervously. He'd spoken mostly to himself, but Brogan, who stood nearby, had heard his words.

"Ya got no head for heights, Neely?" Brogan asked. "You'd best conquer your fears, lad. When we get 'round to busting ourselves out of here, we can't have you slowin' us down. Right, m'lord?" Lute raised his head from the chessboard and smiled at his two companions. He liked it that the pair of them, as different as they were, enjoyed joshing with each other.

"Busting ourselves out of here?" Neely responded. "Are you crazy? How we gonna do that, big fella? We sure ain't a-goin' outta this window, are we? And we surely ain't a-goin' out through that thick, bolted, well-guarded door. I can hear them guards a-mutterin' out there right this minute. So what are we going to do, my friend? Sprout wings and fly off over the castle roof like a trio of ravens or corbies? Maybe Lute can whip up a magic potion and turn us invisible. Then we could slip out when those women bring us our food."

"Never you fear, Neely, Lute'll think o' somethin'. Right, m'lord?"

"I will. Just as soon as I figure out how to save my queen. When I've done that, I'll work on finding us a way out of here."

"Lute, your poor queen ain't got a prayer," Neely said. "M'lord, she's a goner."

You are right, Neely, Lute thought, she hasn't got a prayer—nor do we, most likely. But he kept that thought to himself.

Twice a day for the last three days the women had brought Lute and his companions their meals—such as they were—at mid-morning and then again in late afternoon. On the afternoon of their third day there, something odd happened as the women were leaving. The taller of them, the one who'd given Brogan a shy smile, hesitated for a moment until her companion had gone out through the door. Then she dug down into an apron pocket and pulled out a small cloth-wrapped packet. She handed it to Brogan, then quickly stepped out of the chamber. The guards shut and bolted the door behind her.

When Brogan opened the packet, he saw that it contained two tallow candles, a small steal knife, and a piece of flint. He smiled. It appeared he'd made a friend.

"M'lord," Brogan called out to Lute, who was inside the inner room, "you need to take a look at what I have here."

"Goodness sakes," Lute said, seeing what Brogan was holding, "you have women bringing you gifts?"

"Must fancy you, that tall lass," Neely said, grinning.

"Well," Brogan replied, "I rather fancy her."

The next day when the women were leaving, the taller one again let her companion go out before extracting another small packet from her pocket. This time it contained three small apples and several strips of dried meat. As the woman handed the packet to Brogan, her hand touched his, and at the same time they exchanged smiles. Did he imagine it, or had she also given him a wink before disappearing through the door?

"My lord," Brogan called out to Lute, "here be God's plenty."

"Her name, Brogan, tell us her name," Neely said.

"I ain't got that far just yet," Brogan replied, blushing. The big man was pleased but embarrassed.

❖

Wat's grandson, Simon, was a pudgy, tow-headed little fellow, round of face, with huge, brown doe-eyes. When Wat brought him up to the manor house late on Friday afternoon, they were both welcomed warmly by Jillian, Matthew, and Editha.

"You must stay and share our evening meal," Jillian said, a statement, not a question.

"That be all right by you, Simon?" Wat asked the boy. The boy, having sniffed the aroma of pot roast, nodded his approval.

"C'mon, Simon," Matthew said, "I'll show you 'round while the food's still preparin'. You like horses? We got a pony might be just right for you."

The boy's big eyes got even bigger. "A pony? For me to ride? Grandfather, would that be all right?"

"If'n it's all right with the Lady Jillian, it be all right with me."

"Lute gave Matthew a new, larger pony for his last birthday," she said. "His old one might suit Simon perfectly."

"His name's Stumpy," Matthew said. "He's pretty easy-goin', for a pony."

The boys dashed off toward the stable, Editha following, trying to keep up.

"Any news, my Lady?" Wat asked, when the children were out of earshot.

"Just a few rumors. Mostly about the King, and also, the queen."

"What do they say?"

"Some folks are claiming that the King has been killed, others that he's now on his way back. Nobody seems to know for sure. And the queen, they say, has fled the city for some reason. They say she's gone to earth in the Tower of London."

"That's kinda what I've picked up, too, m'lady. If'n there's any truth to 'em, it's like to stir up that evil fellow Mordred real good. As if he needed any stirrin' up. M'lady, it's all the more reason for us to get Matthew to a safe place. He should be all right with me for a bit, but we'd best try 'n' come up with a more permanent arrangement."

"Why don't we wait until we've heard from Lute," Jill said. "But please don't think I'm questioning your wisdom, Walter. I appreciate your counsel."

After dinner that evening, Matthew, with a bag his mother had packed for him, went off with Wat and Simon to Wat's small dwelling, only a couple of miles to the north of the manor. The boys rode out through the gate on the two ponies, Stumpy and Swifty, Simon looking pleased as anything.

As Jill watched them go, she felt a sinking feeling in her heart. She pulled Editha close to her and held her tight. Lute was gone and now Matthew. But maybe not for long. She knew she shouldn't give up hope about Lute. And maybe the King *would* soon return. As for Lute, he *had* to return. If he didn't, she would die.

❖

Mordred was usually masterful at hiding his emotions, especially his anger. Rather than give vent to his feelings, he tended to keep them well out of sight, and as a result, he simply seethed with an inner fury. His act of hurling the cup of wine across the room, in Lute's presence, wasn't like him. It had embarrassed him. He would do better, he told himself. He mustn't act like a petulant child. He must control himself.

So, his mother had been right about the queen. She was *gone*. But the queen's treachery, Mordred told himself, simply proved that she wasn't worthy of him. Well, he thought, the hell with her. He wouldn't even make an effort to bring her back. She could rot in the Tower of London, for all he cared.

As for Sir Kay and Sir Bedivere, *their* treachery couldn't be ignored. Those bastards had better beware. They would pay a high price for their disloyalty. Those two would pay with their lives.

"Sire?" said Osmond, Mordred's chamberlain, his voice coming through the slightly cracked doorway. "Sir Colgrevaunce is here."

"Cole!" Mordred shouted. "Come in, my friend, come in!" It would be good to see Colgrevaunce, Mordred thought. He was one of the few people who had always been unwaveringly loyal to him. Within days of Mordred's initial arrival in the city, over a decade ago, the two of them had bonded firmly. Cole wasn't like those bastards, Sir Kay and Sir Bedivere. Cole had never let him down.

"Sire," Cole said, "just wanted to be sure you knew

that Lute and his companions are securely where you wanted them. Snug as bugs in a rug, they are. All locked in, guards posted at all times."

"Well done, Cole, well done. Actually, my friend, I've already had a little chat with Lute. My word, he's still the same old Lute, isn't he? I doubt if he gave you any trouble at the manor or on the road."

"Oh, no, sire, not a bit. He's a gentle fellow. But his family was certainly sad to see us haul him off like that."

A gentle fellow? Mordred said to himself, running his hand over his deeply scarred chest. Yes—but not always! Then Cole's last statement finally sunk in.

"His *family?* Lute has a *family?*"

"Oh, yes. A lovely, rather sad-faced, wife, and a young son and daughter."

Mordred sat quietly for a long moment, his pointer finger held against his lips. "A young son," he finally said softly.

"Yes, probably about eight or nine."

"Hmm," Mordred said, "it's odd that I hadn't given any thought to that possibility before. But now I think about it, it's rather obvious, isn't it? Cole, I think we should be including Lute's son in our future plans. I'm sorry, but I may have to send you right back there to Sanham to scoop up that lad and bring him here. Let me think just a little bit more about that, but that does seem likely."

"Happy to oblige, sire, if that's what you'll be wanting."

Chapter 6

In the dark hours of the night, a small, rather rotund figure slowly ascended the city's several long flights of central stairsteps, from the lowest tier to the highest. If anyone had noticed him, they would probably have assumed it was just some sleepy lad making his way up to the citadel, turning up for his late-night duties in the castle stables—or some such thing.

In fact it was Tom, his chubby appearance the result of the long rope hidden beneath his jacket. Mary had wound it a great many times about Tom's slender torso, and it had taken her nearly five minutes to encase him in the seventy-five feet of sturdy rope. Then she'd borrowed one of her father's larger garments with which to cloak his enlarged figure.

The guards at the entrance to the castle nodded at Tom as he passed through. They couldn't have put a name to him, but he wasn't unfamiliar to them. The pudgy, solitary, sleepy-eyed lad gave them no cause for concern.

Tom disappeared into the depths of the castle stables. Ten minutes later, with the coil of rope re-wound aslant from atop his left shoulder to around the right side of his waist, Tom was scaling a drainpipe from a rooftop gutter on the western section of the keep, his small moving form virtually invisible in the darkness.

It took him a few minutes to get his bearings, up amongst the castle's many chimneys and finials, but he knew the section of the keep he wanted to get to, and eventually he reached it. He secured one end of the rope firmly around a chimney pot and tied the other end around his waist.

Neely heard the tapping. It seemed to be coming from outside the shutters to Lute's window.

"Lute," he said, "did you hear that?" Neely got up from the table where he and Lute were playing chess by candlelight and stepped over to the window. There came the tapping again. This time Lute did hear it. He quickly stepped to the window and raised the hook that secured the two shutters together. He pulled back the inner shutter and pushed out the outer one. A face peered in. It was Tom.

The agile young man passed through the narrow opening with ease. He held firmly to a rope. "Grab ahold of the end of this," he said to the astonished Neely, "soon's I've untied it from 'round my waist. Don't let go of it."

Hearing the voices, Brogan stepped into the room. "What's all this, then?" he asked.

"Whoa!" Tom said, "*you're* a big fellow! Hadn't quite reckoned on that."

"Does that cause a problem, Tom?" Lute asked.

"Well, it will be tough enough for *you* to get through the window, Lute. Don't think there's any chance *he* can."

"Then I'd best stay behind," Brogan said. "Anyway, if all of us were gone, they'd know it just as soon as the women came with the food. If I keep the inner door closed, I could say you wanted some privacy. Probably fool 'em for a day or two. Give you fellas a chance to get good and clear."

"But what'll happen to you when they find out?" Neely said.

"I don't think it's me they care about," Brogan replied, "it's the Earl they care about. So, I'm willing ta take my chances. Besides, maybe I have made a friend who might prove helpful in a pinch."

"Well," Tom said to Lute and Neely, "if we're going, we best be going. And what this big fellow is suggesting makes sense. If we can have a day or two's head start before they realize you're gone, we may be away from the city before they unleash their hounds."

"We can't just take off and abandon Brogan," Lute said, "that wouldn't be at all right."

"My lord," Brogan said, "I know you'd sacrifice yourself for me, if'n the tables were turned. So, you'd best get out of here while you can. Be safe, my lord. And you, too, my young friend. Anyway, I should be all right." Brogan clapped each of them on the shoulder. Lute expelled a deep breath. He saw the wisdom in what Brogan and Tom were saying. But he hated abandoning his loyal retainer.

"After I climb back up onto the roof, then it'll be your turn, Lute," Tom said. "Tie the rope 'round your waist. When you feel me give it a light tug, climb on out through the window. You'll be supported by the rope. Use your feet to move yourself down to the corner. There's a very firm drainpipe there which you should be able to climb," Tom added. "The space behind it will give you handholds and toeholds. I'll have a good grip on the rope in case you slip, but you should be able to do it. Neely, once Lute's safely atop the roof, I'll be back for you."

Then, with one hand on the rope, Tom swung himself back out through the narrow opening. He disappeared into the darkness. For a moment they could hear the sound of his feet scrabbling against the wall stones, then nothing.

Two minutes later, Lute felt a little tug on the rope, the signal it was his turn to go. He checked a last time to be sure he had the rope well secured around his waist, then gave Brogan a final farewell gesture. "We'll let my uncle know about you," he said. Brogan nodded his understanding.

Lute squeezed himself through the narrow opening of the window. He clung to the rope with both hands and propelled himself along the surface of the wall with his feet. The night air felt cold against his cheeks. It took only a moment for him to travel the short distance to the corner. He reached out and grabbed ahold of the drainpipe. The lead of the pipe felt cold to the touch. There was a narrow space behind the pipe, and he wedged his toes into it. Then he began to shinny up the pipe. He could see the edge of the roof just ten feet above him. Lute slowly worked his way up. Then, there was Tom's hand reaching down to him. Once he was firmly seated on the roof, his back against a chimney, Lute untied the rope and handed the end to Tom, who quickly secured it about his waist.

"I'll go fetch the lad," Tom whispered. "If he slips, you'll have to hold him, though the end of the rope is also secured around the chimney pot if you can't."

"I'll be prepared," Lute whispered back. "He's nervous, but Neely's really quite able."

"We'll be fine," Tom said. Then he disappeared over the edge of the roof into the darkness.

When Tom climbed back into the room through the window, Neely looked very nervous. "Is this the only way?" he said. "Do I really *have* to do this?"

"Neely, there's nothin' to it," Tom said. "You won't have any difficulties. The rope will hold you, so all you have to do is push yourself along the wall with your feet. When you reach the corner, grab on to the drainpipe. Then pull yourself up it using your hands and feet. I'll be right behind you. Lute will be up above, with a firm grip on the rope." The lad didn't look convinced.

"Neely," Brogan said sternly, "you get your skinny arse out o' that window, or I will kick your skinny arse all the way back to Sanham."

Neely expelled a big breath and nodded. "Big fella," Neely said, "you take care o' yourself, eh?"

Brogan smiled. "I'll do me best, lad," he said.

Neely, with the final few feet of rope securely tied

about his waist, climbed out of the window. Tom watched to see that Neely was moving along the wall just fine. By that point, Tom was so familiar with the handholds in the wall that he didn't really need the rope's support.

All went fine until Neely began to climb the drainpipe. Suddenly there was the sound of rending, as of metal scraping against stone. The pipe was coming loose. "Hell's bells!" Neely cried out in panic.

"Stay still, lad!" Tom called out. "Don't move a muscle! Lute will hold you."

The metal bracket at the top of the pipe attaching it to the wall had failed. The pipe had begun to tilt outward into empty air. In fear, Neely had locked his arms and legs around it. Neither Lute nor Tom could see his face. If they had, they would have seen his look of terror.

"Neely," came Lute's voice from up above him, "I have a firm grip on the rope. Let go of the pipe. I'll haul you up."

The panic-stricken lad had no intention of letting go of the drainpipe. Not until he felt a sharp jab in his behind.

"Do as Lute says, dummy!" came Tom's voice from just beneath him. "He'll pull and I'll push."

"Oh, most Holy Mother," Neely whispered, "please don't forget me in my hour of need." He forced himself to let loose of the pipe—and he fell. A bolt of terror flashed through him.

After a couple of feet, the rope became taut, halting Neely's fall. Then he felt one of Tom's hands pushing against his backside. Finally, quelling his panic, Neely realized he was inching upward against the surface of the wall. Lute was pulling from above, Tom pushing him from below.

After a few agonizingly long moments, Neely saw the edge of the roof coming within reach above him. He reached up and grasped it with both hands. Then he flipped himself up to safety.

Neely lay there, sweating and breathing hard. A moment later, Tom had also climbed over the edge to safety.

Standing above them on the rooftop was Lute. He was shaking out his exhausted arms and stretching them. "Whew," he said, "I'd about reached my limit. Good thing neither of you fellas weighs a whole lot."

"What if we'd fallen?" said Neely, his trembling voice revealing that he was still quite shaken. "What if we'd *fallen?*"

"Not a big problem," Tom said. "The flagstones of that little courtyard down there would have broken your fall."

"You mean they would have broken *me!*" Neely replied, a bit more firmly.

"Aye," Tom said, grinning, "that, too."

"Now what, Tom?" asked Lute.

"Now we catch our breaths, then figure out how to get ourselves out o' this bloody castle with no one a-knowin'."

"Which, I assume, won't be any problem at all, Lute," Neely said, "since we'll be guided by the wisdom of our clever little pal here."

"You learn quick, my friend," Tom replied. "Lute,

I quite like this young man ya brought along with ya. I think ya made a real good choice."

CHAPTER 7

Merlyn couldn't stop thinking about the young woman, her soft dark hair, her deep-set eyes, her slender, supple body. Perhaps that's why he found himself in the predicament he was in.

He had never met anyone like her. Not anyone *close* to being like her. He began to reminisce about their first encounter.

It was springtime, four years earlier, in a leafy forest glade a little higher up the Wye Valley, a place where he loved to go to meditate. On that day the glade had been heady with the fragrance of the wildflowers, the humming of bees, and the springtime melodies of the birds. Merlyn looked up, and there she was, smiling at him, as if by magic.

"May I sit?" she'd asked, in a surprisingly low-pitched voice for someone who looked so delicate. He had simply nodded. He'd watched as she lowered herself to the sward with remarkable grace.

"I'm Nimuë," she said.

For a moment Merlyn didn't reply. Finally, he said,

"Ah, so that's who you are." He nodded his head a few times, then repeated her name. "Nimuë."

"You knew I'd come?" she'd asked, with a tilt of her head.

"Oh, yes. But not where or when."

"It was fated? Written in the stars?"

"No, not in the stars. I don't believe in that nonsense."

"Then where?"

"In here," he said, tapping his chest.

"In your heart?"

Merlyn nodded, his lips compressed.

"*Les plaisirs d'amour* are sweet when they are new," she said.

"So, you know French?"

"Oh, yes. And Latin, of course. My Greek is still rather elementary."

"You know quite a lot for such a young woman. Would you like to know more? Would you like me to teach you?"

"That's why I've come."

"Are you an escapee from a nunnery?" he asked, grinning through his beard.

"Not a nun and not an escapee. I was still a novice when they expelled me from the order."

"And why did they do that?"

"One night they caught me in the library reading the forbidden books. They were most upset."

"Yes, I suppose they were. And why were you reading the forbidden books?"

"Because they were forbidden," she replied, with a

coy smile.

"Ah," said Merlyn, cupping his chin in his left hand.

"Well," she said, as she climbed to her feet, "I'm afraid I must be going. Will you come back tomorrow afternoon to begin my instruction?'

"I will," he replied.

"Yes, I knew you would," she said. "I knew it right here." And she tapped her chest.

As she walked slowly from the meadow, Merlyn heard her low-pitched voice come floating back to him as she sang a plaintive song; *"Les plaisirs d'amour commence en joie, la douleur d'amour dure tout de vie."*

The following day, Merlyn returned to the meadow. As did Nimuë. And the day after that. And the day after that.

❖

Without incident, Lute, Neely, and Tom made a cautious and circuitous descent down from the upper levels of the castle. Following Tom's lead, they ended up in the castle stables, a place Tom knew well from his months of working there. For him, it was something of a safe haven.

"Now we need to split up," Tom whispered. "Getting out of the citadel won't be a problem for me. I can walk straight out through the main gate and the guards won't pay me no mind. For you two, it's gonna be trickier, since it's vital you not be seen. Let me think, what's the best way for you to do it? Hmm."

"Tom, if we can get to the athletic fields somehow," Lute said, "I can guide us safely on from there. I know that area well. Spent quite a lot of time there once."

"Okay, Lute, then how about this? You know the high walkway that connects the castle to the palace?"

"Yes, of course," Lute said.

"Not so very far along it, against the outside wall, there's a tall, slender larch whose branches practically rub up against the stones. There are several trees, but you'll see the one I mean. I'm a-thinkin' you two could use that tree like a ladder. You should be able to climb right down it. That would put you close to them old horse fields o' yours, Lute. This time o' night, the walkway should be quiet and deserted. There'll be guards down at the palace end, o' course, so you'd best creep along the walkway like a pair o' stalking alley cats. Crouch down low and keep close to the outer side of the walkway till ya reach the tree. Yeah?"

"Sounds like a good plan to me, Tom. Okay with you, Neely?"

"How high up is it?" Neely asked nervously.

"No more'n fifty or sixty feet. Nuthin' to it."

" So," Lute said, "after that, we'll meet up in my uncle's back garden. In, say, half an hour?"

Tom nodded. "Ya think he'll be all right with us borrowin' a couple o' his horses?" Tom asked.

"I'm sure he will," Lute said. "He has more horses than he can use these days. He's been after me to take some of them off his hands. This will be my chance to do that."

Neely, who hadn't said much during this exchange, reached out a hand to Tom. "Need ta apologize to ya, my friend. Golly, you really helped us out up there. Sorry I ever doubted ya. Won't never happen again."

"Well, we ain't entirely safe just yet," Tom replied. "But you and me, Neely, we're like to become chums, eh?"

Neely smiled and nodded. "I'd like that."

"Well, hope ta see you fellas in just a bit," Tom said. Then he scurried off.

Lute and Neely crept up the dark, narrow set of steps that led to the walkway linking the main section of the citadel to the royal palace. They crouched there in the darkness, taking a moment for their eyes to adjust and to get the lay of the land. The walkway was dark and empty, but they could hear the muffled voices of the guards down at the far end near the royal palace.

The stones of the curtain wall rose up about fifty feet above the grass. Along both sides of the crenulated walkway, the merlons—the shoulder-high, solid sections of the stonework—extended for about ten feet each. In between the merlons were the crenels, the three-foot high, two-foot wide openings. All along the side of the outer wall stood a row of widely spaced trees. Most of them grew several feet away from the wall.

Peering through the darkness, Lute located the larch Tom had mentioned. It was the third one along the wall. And just as Tom had thought, it was a bit closer to the wall than the others. It was also close to one of the crenels between the merlons.

"Keep down and stay as close to the outside wall as you can," Lute whispered to Neely. "I think we can do this."

Crouched in a low squat, Lute began working his

way slowly toward the larch tree, Neely doing the same behind him. They crept past the first tree and then the second. When they reached the crenel closest to the larch, Lute swung his legs over the three-foot high opening and grabbed onto the nearest tree branch. It was a sizeable branch and it felt firm. Grasping the branch with both hands, he was relieved to find that it took his weight. Then he stretched his legs downward, seeking purchase on a lower branch. He found one quickly. Lute began his slow descent, lowering himself from branch to branch, trying to make as little noise as possible. Many of the smaller branches and larch needles rubbed against his torso and abraided his face as he descended, but in under a minute, Lute dropped down safely onto the ground. Then he pressed his back firmly against the stones of the curtain wall, trying to be as invisible as possible. Above him, Lute could hear Neely climbing over the wall and into the tree.

As he swung his legs over the low opening, Neely found himself struggling against his fear of heights. The events earlier in the evening hadn't helped matters. Now he found himself high up among the branches of the tree, nervously clutching a thick branch, his feet scrabbling for purchase beneath him. With both hands he gripped one of the thicker branches, one Lute had used earlier, a branch he believed should easily hold him, since he was a lot lighter than Lute. Suddenly Neely felt, then heard, the branch beginning to crack. He panicked. Instead of grabbing on to a different branch to support him, he held onto this one for dear life. With a loud crack, the branch snapped. Together, the boy and the branch plummeted.

They crashed down through the lower branches, breaking many of them, then landed on the soft grass with a loud *whomp*. The lad was momentarily stunned. But when he managed to climb to his feet, he felt Lute's hands latch onto him. Lute pulled Neely back against the wall beside him. Neither spoke.

From up above, they heard rapid footfalls. The palace guards had heard the noise and were rushing down the walkway to investigate.

"What in blazes was that?" Lute heard one of them say.

"See anything?" the other one asked.

Then it was quiet for a moment as the two men looked all about, trying to figure out what they'd heard.

"Huh," one of them finally said, "don't see nothin' at all. It's a bit of a mystery."

"No, it ain't no mystery," the other one said. "See that big branch down there. That wasn't there earlier."

"How'd it happen?" the first man asked.

Again, the two men considered the matter for several beats.

"Must've fallen, I guess," the second man said.

"Brilliant," his companion said. "You must be a bleeding genius to have figured *that* out. But why'd it fall?"

"Sometimes dead branches just fall, you know."

"That one don't look so dead to me. Something must've caused it to fall."

"You volunteering to go down there and have a look?"

Then there was another brief silence.

"Hell no. Not me. Anyway, we're supposed to be guarding up here, not down there. I don't think there's anything down there to see. Just some stupid fallen branch. Them lazy grounds fellas can pick it up in the morning. Give 'em something to do."

"Then we'd best get ourselves back to our post."

"Hell, strange noises in the night don't scare me none."

"Yeah, right. You are *so brave*."

❖

The gate to the back garden of Lute's uncle's demesne was firmly closed and bolted, as Lute had expected. Lute stood next to the wall, his legs wide, the fingers of his hands locked together to create a foothold for Neely to step into. The lad did, and Lute hoisted him up to a point where Neely could grip the top of the ten-foot-high wall with his own hands. He vaulted over the wall like a tumbler and landed feet-first on the grass inside the garden—a softer landing than the one he'd experienced half an hour earlier.

"Hold it right there," a voice said softly. Neely looked up with a start.

It was Tom, a foxy grin on his face. Tom reached out and gave Neely a little punch on the shoulder. "C'mon," he said. Neely followed Tom, who moved quickly to his left. He watched as Tom shifted an iron bolt and raised a thick wooden bar. The garden door swung inward, and a second later Lute stepped through.

"How'd *you* get over the wall, Tom, with no one ta

help ya?" Neely asked.

"Oh, lad," Tom replied, "some of us just knows how to do such things."

"Tom's had years of experience," Lute said, with a slight chuckle.

"Bred in the bone," Tom said. "Even Merlyn couldn't take it out o' me. He did try, though."

"Now, you fellows hold it right there!" came a raspy voice from out of the darkness of the garden, startling the three of them. "What you think you're doing?"

"Gwilym," Lute said, "it's me, Lute."

"Master Lute!" cried the old man. He stepped closer, then reached his arms up to Lute and gave him a hug. It was a warmer welcome than the sour little man had given Lute on his initial arrival here, a decade ago. Then, Lute had been totally unknown to Gwilym, and it had taken him a few weeks to win the approval of his uncle's cranky manservant. But when Lute decided to leave the city for good, six months later, Gwilym had been as broken-hearted as anyone there.

Gwilym cast a quick glance at Lute's companions. Neely was new to him, but Tom wasn't. Gwilym had never taken to the little scamp, even though Merlyn, whom Gwilym liked a lot, obviously had a deep affection for Tom. "Well, I'd best go tell the master you're here," Gwilym said. "He'll be delighted."

"No, Gwilym, you mustn't do that. He can't know about us."

"Why's that, Master Lute?"

"When they come searching for us—which they will do, in the next day or so—I don't want my uncle to have to lie to them. I want him to be able tell them honestly he hasn't seen us and knows nothing about us."

"Ah, yes. Now I see. Can I tell him about ya after theys come and gone?"

"Yes, Gwilyn, you may. But first, tell me how my is uncle doing."

"Not so good, Lute. Just all right is about all. Gettin' old, like the rest of us. Juliana takes real good care o' him, and I do what I can. He hates what's been happening in the city, Lute, and he's most terrible worried about the King."

"As we all are, Gwilym."

"But it's mighty good we can hire some help around here. And that's all your doing, Lute." He chuckled softly. "Why, I remembers when you cleared out this whole mess of a garden, all by yourself. Goodness, what a job. And you done it all in just about a week's time, too."

"Gwilym, we need to go. We must be down at the city gates when they open them this morning. We plan on taking two of the horses."

"He'll be glad for that. Them critters are expensive to feed, and we got no one to exercise 'em. I 'member when this here little fella," —he nodded at Tom—"used ta help us out with that."

"Tom," Lute said, "you and Neely go pick out the horses. Gwilym, you think you might find a couple of old cloaks we could take?"

"O' course, Lute. Might you like me to pack a quick bite for yas to take also?"

"Yes, thank you. That would be good. But you must do it quickly."

Without another word, Gwilym turned about and scurried away through the garden toward the back of the house.

The eastern sky was growing light as Lute and Neely, enshrouded in the old cloaks Gwilym had scrounged up, pushed themselves into the midst of the throng of workers waiting to exit the city. Most of the folks there were on foot, though a few rode atop carts or small wagons. Lute and Neely were on foot also, walking ahead of their two horses, holding their reins. Only a few of the others had horses, but Lute believed that he and Neely blended in well enough.

Once more Tom had separated himself from them. The plan was for them to meet up again after they'd all crossed the long bridge above the river. That was the point at which the workers would disperse, many of them to the fields, some to small farms off to the east of the water meadows, and a handful of strong young fellows to the stone quarry over on the far side of the wide valley.

Lute and Tom really didn't look out of place amongst the throng of folks waiting to depart through the gate. But, unbeknownst to Lute, someone watching the gathering had actually recognized him. At least, she thought she did.

Her name was Gwendolyn. A decade ago she had set

her cap for Lute. And at the time the young man had been quite taken with her, too. She'd always aspired to higher things for herself, and the young nobleman had been just what she'd wanted. But it was not to be. And she'd been broken-hearted when she discovered that Lute was suddenly gone from the city. He'd vanished, simply disappeared, and without a single word of goodbye. After a few weeks, Gwendolyn concluded that Lute must be dead—probably killed by the man who was now the Prince Regent of the city—Mordred. In time she'd recovered from her heartbreak, and she'd managed to secure a handsome young merchant for her husband. She now lived with him and her three small children on the city's second level. Not quite on the third level, that of the lesser nobles as she'd hoped, but still a step up from where she'd always been.

But it was down here on the city's lowest level where Gwendolyn still felt most at home, down here where she'd come from. And so, on most mornings she would come here to browse through the stalls and carts that filled the open market square. She'd come down extra early this morning to look over the fruits and vegetables that had just arrived at the tail end of the Harvest.

Gwendolyn stared at the tall man wrapped in the faded blue cloak. She hadn't seen Lute in over a decade, but she felt certain it was him. Her heart was racing, and she realized she was experiencing conflicting emotions. If it really was Lute, then he had left the city without even bothering to explain himself to her. What was he doing?

Why had he been in the city, and why was he leaving now?

Chains began to make grinding sounds, and then the heavy portcullis slowly rose. The crowd of people began to push on through, Lute amongst them.

Was she wrong? Was it just wishful thinking? Could the tall man on whom her eyes remained, really be Lute? It seemed unlikely. But she very much wanted it to be true.

CHAPTER 8

Brogan heard the door being unlatched. He stood across the little room with his back against the closed door to Lute's chamber. The two women entered with the trays of food, and he caught a fleeting glimpse of the guard posted out in the hallway.

"'Scuse me, sir," said the shorter of the women. "Need ta get passed ya."

"No. Just set them trays a-top the stools, if ya don't mind," Brogan said, tilting his head toward them. "They's a-playin' chess in there. The Earl gets a bit irked when I come bargin' in mid-game. Says it breaks his concentration. That food'll keep all right. When they're done, I'll take it in."

The woman shrugged and did as he asked. The taller one shrugged too. As before, she waited a second longer inside the room until the shorter woman had exited. From her apron pocket she extracted a small cloth sack, its opening pulled tight by a string. Her shining eyes were locked onto Brogan's as she handed him the little sack. This time he was the one who offered a wink. The corners of her mouth lifted in a smile.

She scooted back out of the antechamber, the door closing firmly behind her. Brogan waited a moment before he loosened the string securing the mouth of the small sack. Inside, he found a handful of juicy raspberries. He took one out and popped it into his mouth. It was slightly tart, just the way he liked 'em.

Merlyn found himself recalling his second meeting with Nimuë. The afternoon after the day they'd first met, he'd gone to the glade, not sure that she would be there, but hoping she would. He'd been more nervous than he could remember.

She was already there, sitting on the green sward, amongst the tiny, white, wild daisies that grew randomly in the grass. She was wearing a long green flowing skirt and a short-sleeved, white blouse that displayed her slender, pale arms. She looked like a flower among the flowers.

Nimuë looked up at his approach and gave him a mischievous smile. Merlyn gazed into her dark, mysterious eyes. He was entranced.

"I'm so glad you've come," she said in her low, melodious voice. "I wasn't sure you would."

"You didn't know?"

She blushed. "Yes, I did know. I was just trying to be polite."

Merlyn lowered himself down on the grass near her, and for a little while neither of them spoke. Nimuë was looking down at the grass and the tiny white daisies. She was slowly picking them with her right hand and placing them in the palm of her left.

"You asked if I would teach you," Merlyn said. "Where would you like to start?"

"Before we do that, would you mind if I asked an impertinent question?"

"I won't know if I mind until you ask it."

"Merlyn? Is it true what they say about you?"

"And what is it they say?"

"They say that you were the one who managed events leading to the King's conception. They say that it was through your magic that Uther Pendragon slept with the Lady Igraine."

Merlyn ran his hand through his beard. Then he nodded. "Yes, there's probably some truth to that notion."

Nimuë narrowed her eyes and scrunched up her lips, looking thoughtful. Then she said, "Merlyn, tell me about Igraine. Was she very beautiful?"

"Oh yes, she most certainly was."

"More beautiful than me?" she asked, with a tilt of her head.

Merlyn hesitated a moment before replying. "Well, that's not really a fair question. She was very lovely then, and you are very lovely now."

Nimuë's dark eyes focused intensely on Merlyn's. "Merlyn," she said slowly, giving emphasis to each of her words, "did you desire her?"

Merlyn paused for a moment, inhaling slowly before expelling a deep breath. "It was Uther who desired her," he said.

"Yes. But didn't you desire her, too?" she asked, her head tilted again.

"That's another unfair question."

Nimuë tossed the tiny daisies she'd collected in her hand up into the air, and then reached out and tried to catch them, only getting a few. She looked at Merlyn. "Your reluctance to answer tells me that you did," she said.

"Truthfully, *every* man desired her," Merlyn said.

"Well, if *every* man desired her," she replied, "that would include you."

"Yes," he said, conceding the point, "I suppose it would."

"Merlyn, you seem uncomfortable. Do I make you uncomfortable? I'm not really dangerous."

Oh, yes you are! he thought, though he kept the words to himself.

"Come," she said. "Lay your head in my lap. I want to make you comfortable."

Merlyn did as she asked.

"Now close your eyes, and I will sing to you." Nimuë began running her fingers through his gray, wispy hair.

"That feels nice, doesn't it?" she said.

"Umm," he murmured.

Nimuë began to sing to him in her soft, low-pitched voice. It wasn't long before Merlyn had fallen into a deep sleep.

When he awoke, Nimuë was gone. Merlyn was alone in the glade, and the evening's chill was coming on.

❖

The three men were mounted on two of Lute's uncle's horses, Lute on one, Tom and Neely together on the other. They trotted side by side for a short distance until they'd reached the small farm where Tom had left Raguel.

"About time, Tom!" shouted the farmer as they rode up. "I don't know what that blamed critter you left with us is, but he's gone and spooked all my livestock—and me, too. I want him out of here *now*. Take that devil someplace far away, Tom. Don't ever bring 'im back here. I won't have it."

Tom reached into his money pouch, jingling some coins. He extracted three bright and shiny gold pieces. "This be about right, Lum? Hope it suffices. It's all I got right now."

The man's eyes widened at the sight of the coins. "Aye, Tom, them'll suffice. But please, get that damnable monster out o' here. Hope ta Goodness I never set eyes on 'im again."

"Might not be necessary, Lum," Tom said, "but I's most grateful to you."

Raguel was already saddled and rarin' to go. Tom, holding the reins in his left hand, stepped into the stirrup and swung his right leg high over the back of the tall stallion. The horse pranced a step or two sideways and tossed his head. Then he began to lope away. Lute and Neely, already mounted on the other two horses, followed in Raguel's wake.

The three men hadn't yet determined precisely where they planned to go, but it appeared that Raguel was going to make that decision for them. Tom, knowing the horse well, wasn't about to tell Raguel anything different. So for half an hour the three of them rode eastward at quite a fast pace. Finally, Tom tugged hard on his reins and brought the reluctant stallion to a halt. He knew the other horses couldn't maintain such a fast pace any longer and needed a breather.

"So, what's our destination?" Neely asked Tom.

"I did have a place in mind," Tom said. "But Rags seems to have something else planned for us. I learned long ago it's always wise to let this here fella have his way when he's dead set on sumpthin'. Merlyn learned that, too."

"Oh, yes," Lute said, "Raguel does have a mind of his own. And he usually knows what he's doing. I speak from experience." The horse snorted and tossed his head.

"How're your horses holding up?" Tom asked.

"Doin' all right," Neely said. "Can't keep up with Raguel, though."

"Never knew no horse that could. I'll try 'n' hold 'im back a bit, but he seems damned eager to get some place or other."

An hour later they found themselves approaching the upper reaches of the Wye Valley. Raguel led them off to the right, and they were soon moving southward along the right side of the swift-flowing river. Now the horse slowed his pace and ambled more leisurely for the next few miles. He clearly had a destination in mind, though neither Tom nor Lute knew what it might be.

Everything about the powerful black horse mystified

Lute. He remembered that day, more than ten years ago, when the creature had first appeared to him. Lute had found him saddled and bridled and rider-less in a beautiful meadow. After searching unsuccessfully for the horse's owner, Lute had been forced to take the horse with him. He remembered how upset Merlyn had been at discovering that Lute had spent an entire day in the company of the mysterious creature. Merlyn seemed to think that Lute's association with the horse would harm him. Had it? Not so far as Lute was aware. Merlyn mystified Lute almost as much as the horse did. Where was Merlyn now? What had happened to him? Not even Tom knew.

Suddenly Raguel swung to the left. He plunged straight into the river. Tom, taken unawares, held on tight. Lute and Neely pulled up and watched as Raguel pushed deeply into the water. But not so very deeply, as it turned out. Raguel had found a shallow fording place and the water only arose to just above the horse's knees. Lute and Neely spurred their mounts into the river, the water splashing up to their thighs. Soon they'd all crossed to the hillier side of the valley.

There was no path, and Rags moved slowly, winding his way through clumps of trees and shrubs. Finally, he halted. He raised his head and seemed to sniff the air. He snorted, then he gave a loud whinny.

Lute made a quick study of the area around them. He didn't see anything unusual about it. Then, just behind a clump of low bushes, he saw an opening in the hillside beneath an overhanging ledge. Perhaps it was a small cavern.

Could *this* be where Raguel had wanted to take them?

CHAPTER 9

Brogan looked up at the sounds of someone unbolting the door. The women again entered with their food trays. Brogan put his back to the door of the inner chamber, blocking their access.

"Outta the way," barked the shorter woman.

"Can't do it," Brogan replied. "Chess game's in progress."

"Move," she said. "We're goin' in."

"Ain't movin'," Brogan replied, "not whiles the game's goin' on."

"Then we'll hafta move ya," she said. She gave a loud whistle between her teeth, and a moment later two guards came into the chamber.

"You needin' something?" one of them asked.

"Move this lummox outta the way," the woman said. "He don't want ta let us in."

Brogan held his hands out to his sides, shrugged, and stepped out of the way. He reached behind him and pushed the door open. The shorter woman stepped through. Then she let out a shriek. The guards charged past Brogan into the room.

"What the hell!" one of them yelled. "Where are

they?"

"They're not *there?*" Brogan asked, the picture of innocence. "They was right in the middle of their chess game." On the table, the chess pieces were laid out, a game apparently in progress.

One of the guards stepped to the window and threw open the shutters. He craned his neck this direction and that. As far as he could tell, nothing looked amiss. He didn't notice that a drainpipe, fifteen feet to his left, leaned outward from the corner. "Huh," he muttered.

There weren't many places in the two small rooms to check, but the guards and the women peered beneath the beds and looked up the chimneys inside the two fireplaces. Clearly, Lute and Neely were gone. "Oh, hell!" said one of the guards. Both of them, and the shorter of the two women, looked pretty scared. The taller woman gave Brogan a sidelong glance, her eyebrows raised.

"They couldn't have gotten out while *we* was on duty," one of the guards declared. "Must've got out during night somehow when them other fellas was on duty. Can't be *our* fault. Well, we'd best let the sergeant know, eh?"

"Yes, we'd better. But why don't you be the one to tell 'im, since you outrank me."

"Yeah, yeah, all right. What'll we do about this here yokel?"

"We'd best lock 'im in good while we go and report the bad news."

"And hope to hell he don't go a-vanishin' too afore we can get 'im moved down to the donjon. He sure won't be vanishin' from down there."

"Maybe the Prince would enjoy having a little session with 'im, you know what I mean?"

"Ha, ha. I'm sure he would."

"I could stay and keep an eye on him," the taller woman volunteered.

"Good idea. But you'd best wait outside. Keep your ears peeled, eh?"

"I'll do that," she said. "Why don't you leave the keys with me, case I need to get in."

"No, no, we can't do that. Keys can't be 'trusted to nobody but guards. But we can just bolt and bar the door good. Then, if'n you need to get in, you won't need no keys."

The shorter woman gave the taller one a suspicious glance before traipsing off with the two guards to tell the higher-ups their tale of woe.

The tall woman stood outside the door wrestling with her thoughts. Should she release him? It would be easy. Just pull back the latch and unbar the door. But then what? Could she hide him? But where? If he tried to escape and they caught him, they would torture him for sure. That would be horrible. Better to leave things as they were and hope for the best.

Then the pair of guards returned. They opened the door and beckoned to Brogan. As he moved out into the passageway, his eyes and the eyes of the taller woman met. There was meaning in the looks they exchanged.

❖

Old Wat enjoyed having the two lads. Simon was a bit of a lump, but some of Matthew's energy seemed to be rubbing off on him. The boys stayed busy, riding the ponies and performing small chores about the farmstead. Wat's two sturdy helpers showed them how to milk the goats and muck out beneath the chicken coop. In the evenings, the boys plunged into the stream that flowed at the bottom of the cow pasture, frolicking in the water as they washed off the day's grime.

On the morning of the third day, Wat had the boys sit down at his kitchen table where he'd laid out all of his wood carving tools, including a special set of sharp knives, several small chisels, and a spoon gouge. He explained how to use each tool and then demonstrated on a pine slat. He'd prepared several slats of green wood for them to learn on—green wood being easier to carve than hard wood, and pine being softer than most. Maybe, in time, they could advance to sturdier woods such as oak or black walnut.

Those first few days at the little farmstead were idyllic, both for the boys and for old Wat. But Wat knew this could only be a temporary safe haven for Matthew. He knew that he would soon have to come up with a better plan for the lad's long-term safety. At the moment, he didn't know what that might be. But he knew that once the Prince Regent's men came to the manor looking for the boy, it wouldn't take them long to find him here.

"Well, Mags," the shorter woman said snidely to her

companion, as the group accompanying Brogan began to move along the passageway outside the chamber, "I guess this solves the little matter of your *friend* here." The taller woman just ignored her.

Brogan had overheard the little conversation, and before the group of them dispersed, he'd whispered to the woman, "Is your name Maggie?"

"Magdalene," she'd whispered back.

"I'm Brogan," he said softly. She nodded her understanding.

The guards shackled Brogan's hands and then set off, leaving the women behind. They descended through the back passages of the castle, making their way slowly down to the donjon. As they progressed, Brogan's guards took pleasure in shoving and jostling him roughly. Eventually they reached their goal, the citadel's deepest pit. They chucked their prisoner into his cell like he was nothing but a piece of rubbish.

Brogan had the dark, dank cell all to himself. It was a dreadful place. But always a stolid fellow, Brogan didn't despair. Lute would eventually come for him, he believed. Or maybe Magdalene would manage to help him somehow. Anyway, at least one good thing had come from his being brought here: he now knew the taller woman's name was Magdalene.

❖

An alert had gone out for Lute. A reward of 20 crowns was offered for information that led to his apprehension. Constables had searched Earl Thomas's demesne top to bottom, bottom to top. Guards were posted at the city's main gate and at each of the smaller postern gates.

The poor fellows who'd been on duty the night when Lute and Neely disappeared now occupied a cell in the donjon not far from the one where Brogan resided.

Sir Agravaine had taken charge of the search for Lute in the city. Sir Colgrevaunce, with a sizeable contingent, was already en route to Sanham. It wasn't likely they would find Lute there, but they could find his son. The men had strict orders to bring the boy back, unharmed, to the city, as soon as possible.

Chapter 10

Nearly all the dukes, earls, and lesser nobles in the city were assembled in the castle's great hall. Mordred sat at the center of the high table flanked by several of his highest-ranking knights. Mordred's mother, the Queen of Lothian, wasn't present, but next to him at his right sat his brother, Agravaine. Mordred had called them all together for a lavish banquet to celebrate the Feast of Saint Luke. It was October 18th.

As the meal wound down and servers cleared away the dishes from the long side tables, a small group of men entered the hall. The group consisted of three guards and Brogan, whose feet and hands were shackled. Guards flanked him on both sides and another guard followed behind, prodding him in the back with the blunt end of his halberd. They advanced slowly toward the dais. When they arrived there, Brogan stood with his eyes directed downward at the colorful floor tiles.

No one in the hall knew what Mordred intended by summoning this unknown prisoner before them. Maybe it was to provide some sort of grim entertainment? If so, most of them dreaded it. Some, however—men more like-minded to the Prince himself—relished the possibility.

"What is your name?" Mordred asked the man who stood before him. Mordred's outwardly pleasant demeanor surprised many of the nobles.

The prisoner's head came up and his eyes met Mordred's. "I'm called Brogan," he said. Brogan showed no hint of fear.

"You are the Earl of Sanham's man?" Mordred asked.

"I am, m'lord. And I'm proud to serve 'im. He's a good man, the Earl of Sanham."

Mordred smiled. He cradled his chin in his hand. "Do you happen to know where this good man, the Earl, might now be?"

"M'lord, I do not."

Mordred nodded his head slowly. "And did you, Brogan, assist him in his hasty and unauthorized departure from the accommodations we so graciously provided him?"

"M'lord, I did not."

Once more Mordred nodded slowly, as if accepting Brogan's answer. "And would you know how it was he was able to, uh, *extricate* himself from the castle?"

"M'lord. I don't know the word you just used, but if I get your meanin', the answer is that he *extercated* hisself by climbing out through the window."

"Yes, apparently he did. And then what did he do?"

"M'lord, I can't hardly tell you. When I went into his room, he 'n' Neely, why, they was just plain gone. The window in there was open, and they was gone. I never set eyes on 'em again."

"So, Brogan, you are averring that *you* had no part in the Earl of Sanham's escape. Is that what you are claiming?"

"M'lord, I ain't a-claimin' nuthin'. M'lord, they done it all by theirselves. The Earl didn't get a lick o' help from me. I guess he didn't need none."

Many of the noblemen had begun to smile and chuckle, amused by the plain and rather bold words this man was daring to speak to the Prince Regent. It worried them, though, that his plain, bold words might well rouse the Prince's ire and thus increase the torture they anticipated he would soon be receiving.

"Brogan," Mordred said, looking at the man intensively, "how loyal would you say you are to the Earl?"

"Loyal as the day's long, m'lord."

"Would you lie to protect him?"

"M'lord, I ain't a-lyin'. I be a truthful man."

"How loyal would you say you are to Britain?"

"M'lord, I would give my life's blood for Britain."

Mordred rose slowly to his feet. He smiled as he looked out at all the nobles gathered there. He spread his arms out wide and then loudly proclaimed, "It seems to me that this man has given us some very good and honest answers. Brogan," he said, now looking down at the man standing before him, "I believe you. I applaud your loyalty to your lord and to your country. Should Britain ever have need of your service, I trust that you will be willing to take up arms against our foes."

"M'lord, I shall."

"Provost, remove the shackles from this man. Return

his horse to him and his belongings. This brave man is free to go. Britain needs men like him."

With one voice the nobles raised a spontaneous and heart-felt cheer. The Prince Regent's magnanimous behavior had surprised them, but it had pleased most of them. Perhaps Mordred wasn't quite the villain many of them had taken him for.

Amidst their cheering, many of the nobles had breathed great sighs of relief. Many, but not all. There were some there who had hoped to see some entertainment of a violent sort. Those men were greatly disappointed.

As the late afternoon sun gave color to the edges of the clouds that hovered above the tall towers of the citadel, two women stood and watched as a lone horseman crossed the central square of the city's lowest level. He trotted toward the main gate.

The two women were friends. They had just finished their day's labors up at the castle and were on their way back to their homes. One of them was named Mary and the other Magdalene, a coincidence that people often found amusing. The man they watched was Brogan. He passed through the gate and was soon beyond their sight. A moment later, a second horseman rode across the square toward the city gate.

"He's being followed," Mary whispered.

"Yes. But he's a capable fellow. I think he can take care of himself." Magdalene hoped she was right.

As Magdalene's thoughts lingered on Brogan, Mary found herself wondering where her own fella, Tom, might be.

❖

"Merlyn," Nimuë had said one day as they'd been finishing a lengthy discussion about the uses of charms and spells, "would you show me where you live? Since you come here by foot, it surely can't be far."

"I'm quite a good walker," Merlyn replied. "I have ridden a horse, but only one. And that blasted creature was the very devil himself." Nimuë laughed.

"I can't picture you on a horse, Merlyn."

"Nor can I."

"But tell me, Merlyn, where do you live? There are no villages nearby. Not even a hamlet. Do you have a cottage tucked away somewhere? You surely don't live in a tree, do you? I do wish you would show me."

Merlyn scratched his beard. "Well, I do live fairly close by. But it's my very own special, private refuge. No one else has ever been there."

"Your special refuge? But Merlyn, aren't I special?" she asked coyly.

"Oh, yes," he said. "Well, hmm, let me think about it." I knew this time would come, Merlyn said to himself. But I'm not ready for it yet.

"If I took you there," he said, "you would probably just go poking about in all my secret treasures, my magic amulets and such. And you'd probably be sticking your nose into all my forbidden books. All you would do is make trouble for me."

"Yes, very likely." Then they both remained quiet for a moment.

"Merlyn, you said you've only ridden one horse. Tell me about that horse."

"Ah. Raguel."

"Is that really his name?"

"I don't know. But he responds to it. I did try a number of others, but he didn't seem to like any of them."

"What does Raguel look like?"

"He's a huge black stallion with three white socks. He can run like the wind. When you ride him, you never know where you will wind up because that devil goes where he wishes. He's an independent creature. I've seen him do some quite dubious things, Nimuë, and I've also seen him do some most amazing things."

"Sounds a lot like you," she said.

"Yes, I suppose so. That's one of the things that worries me about him."

"How was it you came to ride him?"

"That's a tale for another day. For now, let me just say that I rode him in order to prevent a friend of mine from riding him. It was the first time I'd ever been on a horse. I can't say it was a pleasant experience for me."

"Why didn't you want your friend to ride him?"

"To keep him from being corrupted."

"Corrupted by a horse?" she asked, with a tilt of her head.

"That's what I thought at the time. Nimuë, Raguel is

not just some ordinary horse."

"But what about you? Weren't you afraid of being corrupted if you rode on him?"

It was far too late to worry about that, Merlyn thought to himself.

"Me worry about being corrupted?" he said aloud. "Surely you know by now that I am incorruptible."

"Ha, ha, ha," she laughed, and her laughter echoed through the glade.

Chapter 11

Mordred looked down upon the city. It was a chilly morning, and wisps of smoke rose skyward from many chimneys. The weak October sun, even when it reached the zenith, would do little to dispel the chill. Winter wasn't far away. Mordred pulled his cloak tightly about him, his mind roaming restlessly.

Last night he'd experienced a most unsettling dream, a dream about King Arthur. In it, he'd seen Arthur and the tattered remains of his army straggling toward a foreign shore. When they arrived there, they'd begun preparing to embark in a miscellaneous assemblage of ships. In his dream, the King looked worn and weary, downcast and discouraged. But he still possessed a sizable force of knights, yeomen, and foot soldiers. The men in the army, as they boarded the raggedy flotilla, looked defeated—but also relieved to be going home.

Could this be true? Could his father still be alive? Could he and the remnants of his army really be returning? Mordred had his doubts. All the reports he'd received indicated that the King's army had been routed, that Arthur—and also his beloved nephew Sir Gawain,

Mordred's half-brother—had been killed. But he didn't know for certain. He had to know.

If the King really was coming back, he must be thwarted. In the last year, Mordred's own army had been molded into an impressive force. As Mordred reflected on the matter, he knew that, to be on the safe side, he'd better mobilize several of his finest units and position them where they could repulse any attempts of King Arthur to land on British soil. He also had to make sure the coastguards in all the coastal watchtowers were fully alerted.

❖

Raguel whinnied loudly and pawed the earth. Lute stared at the strange opening in the hillside. He sensed movement from inside of it.

"Tom?" came a voice, sounding as if it were very far away. "Is that you?"

"Sir," Tom shouted, "it is. Sir, it's me 'n' Lute."

Raguel whinnied even more loudly.

"And o' course Rags, sir. And Neely, too—though you may not know Neely. But sir," Tom went on, "where be ya? Can't see ya, sir. Are ya back beneath that there overhang?"

"No, you can't see me, and you can't come to me, either. But what you can do is *listen* to me."

"This is all very strange, sir."

"It is, Tom, even for me."

Raguel nickered again.

"Hello, Rags, you old devil. Brought my friends, did

you? I thought you knew no one was ever allowed to come here."

Rags gave a loud snort.

"Yes, well, you do what you want, don't you, despite what anyone else may want."

Rags snorted again.

"I'm glad you brought them, Raguel. You knew it was important."

"Sir," Lute said, speaking for the first time, "what can we do to help you? Rags must've known you needed help. That must be why he brought us here."

"You can't help me, Lute. There's only one person who can help me, and I doubt if she wants to. But I can help *you*, which is probably why Raguel brought you here."

"How can you help us, sir?" Neely asked, wanting to be a part of things.

"If you would all just be quiet a moment and listen to me, I might be able to tell you," Merlyn said, sounding grumpy. Raguel snorted.

"You be quiet too, Rags. Listen, Lute, something terrible's about to occur in Sanham. I don't know what it is, precisely, but you must go there and prevent it from happening."

"Is it Mordred? Does he mean harm to Jillian?'

"Yes, it's Mordred. But not Jillian. Lute, tell me, who else is there?"

"No one. Only Jill and my children, Matthew and Editha."

"Ah, of course, Lute, your *son!* I can be so thickheaded

sometimes. I'd forgotten, Matthew. That must be it."

"Sir, what should we do?" Tom asked.

"Go! Go now, Tom! Get to the boy before Mordred does. Hide him! There's not a moment to lose. Mordred's henchmen are probably on their way there now. Rags, you must fly like never before! You must save the boy!"

Raguel whinnied, as if in reply.

"But what about you, Merlyn?" Lute said, concerned about his old friend.

"Don't worry about me, Lute, I'm not going anywhere. But you must hurry. Save the boy. And when you've done that, you must go and save the King!"

"The King?" Lute asked. "What about the King?"

"He'll need you, Lute. But first, go and save the boy! Now *Go*."

And so they did.

❖

Willikyn and Eldred watched as the band of horsemen drew up before the main gate of the manorial compound.

"Open the gate!" boomed Colgrevaunce's loud voice. "We're here at the behest of the Prince Regent. *Open up*."

Eldred started to lift the heavy bar, but Willikyn reached out and stayed his hand.

"Sir," Willikyn said, "it'll just take a moment to inform her ladyship of your visit."

"Open the gate *now*," Colgrevaunce shouted, but Willikyn had already turned about and was scurrying toward the manor to warn the Lady Jillian.

"You!" Cole said sternly to Eldred, "open this gate

immediately—if you know what's good for you."

Eldred dithered for a moment, then began to unbolt and unbar the gate as ordered.

Colgrevaunce and his men rode into the enclosure and crossed the open space toward the manor house. Jill, having just been forewarned, stepped out onto the covered gallery. She watched as the troupe of riders gathered beneath her.

"The earl isn't here. He has gone to the city," she said, looking down at Colgrevaunce. "I believe, sir, you are the one who accompanied him there."

"M'lady," Cole said, "where are your children?"

"Children? I have only a daughter. She is inside, busy with her studies. Would you like me to call her?"

"Yes, please, if you would."

"Editha," Jillian called out, "these men would like to meet you."

The shy little girl peeked her head out, then cautiously came out onto the gallery and stood at her mother's side. Jillian pulled her close against her, her arm about her waist.

"Your name is Editha?" Cole asked her.

She nodded.

"How old are you, Editha?"

The little girl held up both hands, her right hand showing five fingers, her left one finger. "Six," she said softly.

"Editha, how old is your brother?"

Editha was about to answer when she felt the pressure

of her mother's arm. She hesitated, then shrugged.

"Where is he, Editha?"

Again, she shrugged.

"Do you know what happens to little girls who lie?"

Editha remained silent.

"The bogeys come for them."

"Don't worry, Editha," Jill said, "he's only teasing. You are not a liar, and the bogeys don't really exist."

"I'm sorry, m'lady, but if you refuse to tell us where your son is, we will need to make a thorough search of the manor." Without waiting for Jill's reply, Colgrevaunce began issuing orders for his men, in groups of two, to start their search of the entire manorial compound.

❖

It had taken Brogan two and a half days of hard riding to reach the outer reaches of the lands belonging to the Earl of Sanham. He knew he'd been followed, but he felt sure he wouldn't be leading his pursuer to Lute. Lute would surely have gone to ground somewhere far from his own home. But now Brogan had to decide what he should do— just go home to his own little farm? Or should he go first to the manor house to check on her ladyship? Or, maybe, he thought, he should make a last-minute attempt to ditch his pursuer, just to confound the fellow. Yes, that's what he would do—for the simple pleasure it would give him, if for no other reason.

At the moment, he was close to what they'd always called "the Puzzle Wood," a hilly and thickly wooded grove of trees with a welter of confusing, almost labyrinthine, paths. It was a place Brogan knew well. He had often played there as a child. It was a place where he could lose his pursuer with ease.

Half an hour later, Brogan emerged from the confusing grove, a big grin on his face. And there before him stood a horse and rider. What in the world?

But the rider wasn't his pursuer. It was Tom, perched atop a huge black stallion.

"Hail, fellow, well met," said Tom, with a broad smile. "Guess you musta gone and busted out o' that blamed citadel all by yorself."

"Not quite," Brogan replied. "But Tom, what are you doing here? And where's Lute?"

"I was just havin' a look at what's a-goin' on at the manor. The place is crawlin' with the Regent's men."

"Are they searchin' for Lute?"

"Oh, yes. But most especially they're a-searchin' for his boy."

"For young Matthew?"

"Yes, indeed. By the look o' things, they ain't found him just yet, which tells me he must be somewheres else. So, big fella, what we gotta do is figure out where that is. We really gotta find 'im afore they do."

"Well, I s'pose the one who's most like ta know what's afoot is Old Wat," Brogan said.

"Then here's what we do. First, you tell me how to find Wat's farm. I'll go straight there. You ride on back the way I just come and find Lute and Neely. Tell 'em where I'll be. They're a-comin' behind me, like ta be a couple of hours' ride back down this road here to the west. Then all of yas come to Wat's farm. When you do, you gotta make darn sure no one sees ya. Ya got it?"

Brogan told Tom how to get to Wat's cottage.

"I got it, big fella," Tom said.

"Good," Brogan replied. "Then I expect I'll be seein' ya later tonight. Say, Tom," he went on, staring wide-eyed at Raguel, "that's quite some horse you got there."

Rags tossed his head.

"Aye," Tom replied, "you're right, this old devil is quite some horse. Now, *go*."

Chapter 12

Jillian knew it probably wouldn't take long for them to discover where Matthew was. She needed to get word to Wat, but since Colgrevaunce's men were lurking everywhere, it wouldn't be easy. She daren't ask Willykin or Eldred to do it. She would have to do it herself. But she would need someone to stay with Editha. She would send for Willykin's wife, Alys, a cheerful woman who loved Editha like the daughter she'd never had, a woman who doted on both Editha and Matthew.

When Alys arrived, Jill had already donned her riding clothes. Then, being sure she wasn't seen, she slipped around behind the barn and into the stables. There she saddled and bridled her favorite filly. Jill was a highly skilled rider. She'd often pitted her skills against Lute when they rode out together, sometimes even besting him.

She didn't lead her horse toward the compound's main gate but slipped around behind the manor house. Then she moved quickly up the sloping hillside toward a small, well-concealed postern gate in the high stone wall. The rarely used gate was overgrown with ivy, as were the flanking sections of the wall. Jill paused, looked all about. Feeling sure she hadn't been observed, she passed through the opening, her horse ducking its head beneath the stone lintel.

Holding the horse's reins, Jill walked for fifty yards into the woods. Then she mounted and began trotting down the forest trail, the sound of the horse's hooves muffled by fallen leaves. Her trail didn't lead in the direction she wanted, but she knew that in half a mile it would intersect with one that would. She stepped up her pace. It shouldn't take more than fifteen minutes to reach Wat's cottage.

"Where's the boy?" the man shouted at Willikyn. He gripped Willikyn's throat with one hand and began to squeeze; he raised his other arm, his hand making a fist.

"Ain't no boy," Willikyn gasped, "there's just the girl." Finally the man loosened his grip and shoved Willikyn away. After putting the fellow through a rough five minutes, he realized he wouldn't get anything out of him. No point in killing him.

The man turned his attention to Eldred. Maybe he would be an easier nut to crack. "Your turn," he snarled at Eldred. "Ya got just one chance ta tell me where he is afore I wring your neck. After that, I'll pull your guts out through your mouth." Eldred stepped back, but he wasn't fast enough to avoid the man's backhanded slap. Eldred tasted the blood at the corner of his mouth and raised one hand to his burning cheek. His fear was palpable. The man grabbed him by his throat.

"Where *is* he!" the man roared. "Tell me now, or *you're for it!*" He raised his fist, but before he could strike the blow, Eldred blurted out, "No, please, don't hit me."

"Then tell us where he is!"

"I'll tell ya, I'll tell ya."

"You shut your gob, Eldred," Willikyn shouted at him.

"He's at the farm," Eldred said, gasping for breath, "that's where he is, Wat's farm. I can take you there, if ya wants. Please, don't hit me." Eldred slumped to his knees, groveling in the dirt before his fearsome interrogator. Willikyn turned away in disgust.

The two boys, Matthew on Swifty, Simon on Stumpy, rode side by side through the farthest corner of the pasture. They'd been riding for several hours, and during all that time, Simon had kept up well. His riding had greatly improved in just a few days.

The late October afternoon was drawing on, and the smell of wood smoke wafted through the air. Matthew knew they'd best be heading back. It had grown chilly, and Matthew, with his free hand reached back and pulled the hood of his dark red woolen cloak up over his head. Simon, whose blue cloak was longer and hung down all the way to his calves, raised his hood also. The boys were eager to get back to the hot meal and cozy fire they knew awaited them. They didn't know they were being watched.

Wat was relieved to see the lads finally return. He didn't like for them to be out quite so late, though he also didn't like fussing at them. He was pleased at how well they were getting along, and also by the fact that the best qualities of one seemed to be rubbing off on the other—Matthew's energy and high spirits exerting an influence on the normally lethargic Simon; Simon's bookishness influencing Matthew, who usually preferred doing to studying.

When the boys entered the cottage, they hung their cloaks on wooden pegs behind the cottage door, washed their hands and faces at the water bucket, then headed for Wat's sturdy kitchen table.

Wat stood at his cook stove, ladling a thick stew into three large wooden bowls. He'd already placed a wicker basket filled with fresh bread on the table. Simon poured cups of milk for himself and Matthew, and Matthew sliced up a couple of apples, then laid them out on a small platter. When they were all seated, the boys bowed their heads. Wat mumbled his way through a little prayer of thanksgiving. "Amen," the boys said in unison.

There came a soft tap at the door. "Wat?" It was Jillian.

"Come in, m'lady!" he called out.

Jillian stepped quickly through the door, her cheeks rosy from riding through the chilly evening air. "Wat, there are men at the manor house looking for Matty. We must hide him." Alarm flashed across the boys' faces, and Wat's face took on a look of ferocity.

Just a moment later there came another tap on the door. The four of them froze where they were.

"Bugger," Wat muttered. The boys were startled by

the unexpected vulgarity.

Jill placed a finger over her lips. There was a long moment of silence.

"Jillian? Wat? It's me, Tom." The small man opened the door a crack and poked his head in. Wat recognized him from the time, long ago, when he'd come there with Merlyn.

"Welcome, lad, welcome," Wat said, breathing a sigh of relief. "Please, come in."

"They're out there," Tom said. "They're like ta be here any minute."

"Where's Lute?" Jillian asked.

"Not so far behind me, maybe an hour or so. But I don't reckon he'll be here soon enough ta help us."

"Tom," Wat asked, "what do you think we outta do?"

"I saw the boys riding in earlier," Tom said. "But I weren't the only one what saw 'em. There's some fellas watchin'. That's good and that's bad. It's good because them fellas'll know the ponies when they see 'em. So, here's what I'm a-thinkin'. If I was ta put on Matt's red cloak and go tearin' off on his pony, they'd think I was Matt. More'n likely, most of 'em would go tearin' out after me. That there's a good pony Matt has. I could lead 'em a merry chase."

Tom's plan drew no response from the surprised others.

"Jill," Tom went on, "ya think you could ride Rags?"

"Tom, there's no horse I can't ride," she replied firmly.

"Mother," Matthew said, "only three people have ever

been able to ride him."

"It's soon going to be four, Matt," she said, with steel in her voice.

"Well, ma'am," Tom said, "that's good. 'Cuz they'll probably leave a few fellas behind ta keep an eye on things here. But if you and Matty are on Rags, you should be able ta catch 'em off guard and rush right by 'em. Once Rags is on the trail, they'll never keep pace with you. You just keep on a-goin' till ya meet up with Lute and Neely."

"And then what?"

"Then you turn Rags over to Lute, and he and Matthew just go."

"Where, Tom? Go where?"

"Go back to his old home, Jill."

"Back to the little hamlet where Lute and I grew up? The place where Lute's mother still lives? Is that what you mean?"

"That's 'xactly what I mean. Lute says he's got a pal there named Rob. Lute thinks Matty would be safest if he stayed with Rob and his own sons."

"Lute and I grew up with Rob," Jill said. "The three of us were the closest of friends."

"Jill," Tom said, "Brogan and Neely will be with Lute, too. After you exchange horses with Lute, you and Brogan make your way back to the manor house. Neely should go with Lute and Matt. You think you can get back to the manor without being seen?"

"I can go back the same way I got here." Tom nodded his approval.

"Goodness, Tom," Wat said, rubbing his chin, "that's some plan ya got there. It might even work, too. But Tom, what about you? If you're riding on Swifty, them fellas will surely catch up to you pretty quick, won't they?"

"Not all that quick. And surely not before Jill and Matthew, ridin' on Raguel, should be able ta get themselves well clear o' the others. Besides, even though they're likely ta find Matt's pony fairly soon, they ain't never gonna find me," he said emphatically. "No, not never."

Suddenly a pony and rider who was wearing a small red cloak burst through the open gate at the rear of the small farmyard. As the pony broke into a canter, the startled watchers looked at their leader for instructions.

"Idris, you and Ewen stay here and keep alert," Colgrevaunce ordered. "The rest of you, go! Catch that lad and haul 'im back. But don't hurt 'im." Six riders spurred their horses and were soon galloping across the open pasture. Colgrevaunce paused for a moment, considering the larger situation, then he, too, set off in pursuit of the others.

By the time he'd reached the far end of the pasture, the small rider wearing the red hooded cloak had a 100-yard lead on his pursuers. He directed his mount off to the left and into a thick copse of beeches. The pony, Tom knew, was low enough to be able to trot unimpeded beneath the branches. The tall men, on their higher horses, would have a harder time navigating through the dense forest.

Although Tom wasn't familiar with the area, his quick

brain nosed out a route that would pose a challenge to the men behind him, yet one that wouldn't confound them entirely. He knew he mustn't lose them. He must keep them on his trail for at least thirty minutes. After that, it should be safe for him to "disappear." By then, Jill and Matthew should have put some good distance between themselves and Wat's farm.

Finally, Tom spotted just the kind of tree he'd been looking out for, a massive beech with many large branches and a surprisingly thick canopy for this late in the year. His pursuers weren't far behind when he leapt off Swifty's back. He quickly shed Matthew's red cloak and scampered up amongst the lower branches of the tree. Moments later, he was high up in the beech where he disappeared from sight in the tree's thick canopy. Good thing, he thought, that beech trees keep their leaves well into late autumn.

The riders were flummoxed. Now they had the pony, and now they had the boy's cloak, but no boy. Where was he?

"Find him!" Sir Colgrevaunce shouted. "Find that little scamp. Spread out. He can't have gotten far."

But after an hour's searching, they hadn't found "the little scamp."

"Well, hell," Colgrevaunce said. "Let's go on back. He's likely to turn up in the morning, glad to see us after freezing his arse off out here overnight. Take his cloak. It'll teach 'im a lesson."

CHAPTER 13

Idris and Ewen were startled by the sound of rapid hoof beats. From out of the shadows of the little roadway leading down to the farm, a huge black horse came charging. The horse, carrying a pair of riders, shot past them in a pounding of hoofs and a blur of movement. The two men, who'd been taken unawares, spurred their mounts and rushed into action.

The pursuers' horses were good, and they were well rested. For the first mile or so they stayed right on Raguel's heels. But soon the superiority of the powerful black stallion began to show, and Jill and Matt stretched out to a comfortable lead.

But after another couple miles, Raguel began to slacken his pace. The big horse was tiring.

"Rags is pretty wore out, Mother," Matthew said nervously. "He musta done a lot of hard ridin' in the last few days."

By then Idris and Ewen had drawn nearly even with the boy and his mother, one on one side, one on the other. Matt's hand slipped down to the knife in his belt. He loosened it in its sheath. It was a modest weapon, but it was all he had. He imagined plunging it into the thigh of one of the riders as they came alongside of them.

"Stop!" Ewen shouted. "We mean you no harm."

Idris stood up in his stirrups and tried to grab ahold of Rag's bridle, but he was thwarted when the big horse suddenly put on a fresh burst of speed. Now Jill and Matt found themselves pulling away again, one length, then two. But it was only a brief reprieve. After another minute, the big stallion, breathing hard, began slowing down once more.

Then, just as the two men had nearly drawn alongside, Raguel sped up again. This time only a little, only just enough to frustrate and infuriate their pursuers.

"You devil," Jill said, addressing the horse, "you're *toying* with them! *And* with us! You can cut it out!" Matt thought he heard the horse give a little snort.

A third time the horse allowed their pursuers to nearly catch them. Then he stepped out with alacrity, displaying his remarkable speed more than ever before.

"Hold on, Matt. I believe that Rags is finally finished with his fun and games."

Indeed, he was. After another quarter of an hour, the men trailed them by a considerable distance. After half an hour, the discouraged fellows abandoned their pursuit altogether.

Now that they were alone, the beast slowed to a trot. "You devil," Jill said again, this time her voice sounding almost affectionate. She reached forward and patted the great stallion's muscular neck. "You knew what you were doing, but I wish you'd deigned to let us in on it."

Rags snorted. He adjusted his pace to a smooth and loping canter, and they glided along for the next several miles in relative comfort.

"Father!" Matt cried out half an hour later. The boy had recognized the pair of riders now approaching along the trail ahead of them—Lute and Neely.

"Jill? Matt? And Raguel? Who would have thought it?" Lute said.

"They tried to take Matt," she said. "But Tom came up with a plan to thwart them."

"I'll bet he did," Neely said with a chuckle. "That little villain sure does have a knack for coming up with a plan, don't he?"

"So what's our plan now?" Lute asked.

"Well, *my* plan," she said, "is for you to take that damnable creature off my hands. I've had more than my fill of this cussed beast."

"Oh, Father," Matt said, "before, only three people had ever ridden Rags. Now it's five! With Mother and me, it's five!"

"A special group, Matt. No surprise your mother's become part of it. As for you, Matt," Lute said, reaching out and tousling the boy's hair, "did the ride frighten you at all?"

"Just a little when those riders nearly caught us. Father, I was ready to fight 'em. But old Rags, he just wouldn't let 'em catch us. Mother is wrong. He's not a damnable creature, he's a wonder." Rags snorted.

As Jill explained Tom's plan to Lute, Neely stepped into the woods and found a stream where they could water the horses. "Over here," he shouted. "Just the place." Soon Matt was scooping up handfuls of water and splashing his face and neck. Raguel plunged his long horse face deep into the stream.

"So, Jill," Lute said, "I guess you know the trail back to the manor, the one that cuts through Cheatham Woods?"

"Yes, I was thinking the same thing. It will be dark, but the moon's coming up, so I should be all right."

Before they mounted, Jillian hugged Matt and then Lute. She gave Raguel a final neck pat.

"Stay safe, Jill," Neely said.

"You too, Neely. You be a-guardin' my menfolk, right?"

"I'm were countin' on them ta be a-guardin' me," he said, grinning.

"Lute," Jill said, "give my warmest regards to Lyonore." She was referring to Lute's mother, a woman for whom she had deep affection.

"Of course," he replied. "And you give Editha a hug and kiss from her father."

The riders turned their horses' heads and went their separate ways.

❖

Colgrevaunce was irked. He and his men had been made fools of. He hated it. He couldn't help wondering who the hell it had been riding on that pony. He'd *thought* that rider had been awfully damned skillful, too damned skillful to be a mere boy. Now Idris and Ewen had returned empty-handed from their long chase. So, they'd been doubly fooled.

"We did our best, sir," Idris said. "But that huge black horse was a marvel. Fastest creature I've ever seen."

"Well, hell," Colgrevaunce said, not for the first time. "Who's still left here at the farm?"

"Just the old farmer and his grandson. I believe his name is Simon."

"That's it, eh?"

But then a devious little notion began to slither into Cole's brain. Well, it was true they'd lost the boy they'd been seeking. But there was still another boy here. And who would know the difference? No one in the city had ever seen Lute's son. Who would know the difference if they turned up with *this* boy instead? Mordred surely wouldn't. Anyway, who could blame them for not bringing the right boy? They had never seen the right boy themselves. To Colgrevaunce, one boy seemed as good as another.

PAWN

SACRIFICE

Chapter 14

Simon and his grandfather exchanged tearful farewells. Wat, terrified about what the future might hold for his beloved grandson, did his best to conceal his fears. Then the boy, mounted on Swifty, departed in the company of Colgrevaunce and his men.

In the morning, Tom made his way back to Wat's cottage on foot. He saw no one during his long walk, and he made sure that no one was lurking about the cottage. Things there were eerily still. So maybe, he thought, their plan had worked. Maybe Jill and Matt's flight on Raguel had drawn Colgrevaunce and his men far away.

Tom stepped up to the cottage door and rapped on it softly. He thought he heard a low groan from inside. He opened the door and slipped in. Old Wat was hunched over his table, his head cradled in his hands.

"Sir, are you hurt?"

Old Wat looked up. He shook his head slowly. "Tom, I don't know whether I'm furious with you or pleased with you," he said.

"Sir, I don't understand."

"They got away, Jill and Matthew."

"So, the plan worked?"

"But Tom, . . . they took Simon."

"What? They took *Simon?* Why would they do that?"

"They needed a boy. He was all they could get, so they took 'im. Now he's gone. My only grandson. Tom, what will I do without Simon? He's my own daughter's only child."

"Oh, sir, I'm terribly sorry."

"What do ya think they're likely ta do ta him? What will Mordred do when he discovers he's not the boy he wanted?"

"I don't know. But it seems to me it's Colgrevaunce who should be in trouble with Mordred, not Simon. But sir, I'll borrow one of Jill's horses and set off for the city at once. I may be able to do some good when I get there."

"I'm sure glad they didn't get young Matthew, Tom, don't get me wrong. The most important thing's the Earl's son. But that poor little mite. He's all the family I got left. Please save the lad—if you possibly can."

"Sir, I'll do everything in my power."

❖

Simon, now alone with these strange, rough fellows, had begun to feel quite fearful. He had no idea why they had taken him or what they intended to do with him. The men, however, were soon impressed by the boy's ability to keep up with them and by the fact that the inherently cheerful little lad offered few complaints.

When the whole party stopped to take a short mid-morning break, Ewen offered the boy some bread and cheese. The boy reciprocated by sharing the bag of walnuts his grandfather had sent with him. There was no doubt that the lad had a good appetite, judging by how eagerly he devoured the bread and cheese, his voraciousness causing the men to laugh. Simon joined in the laughter, and it was then it dawned on him that these men, as rough and uncouth as some of them were, didn't mean him any harm. Indeed, they seemed quite taken by him. Before long, Simon had set most of his fears aside.

During the three-day journey from Sanham to the city, a curious bond formed between the men and the boy. Simon, by nature, was a shy and quiet little fellow, but despite the hard travelling and their sleeping rough, he never griped or whined. Riding on Swifty, not Stumpy, the boy did surprisingly well at maintaining the pace the men wanted to set. They joked about his obvious delight in eating, but they admired the little fellow for never complaining at the meagerness or poor quality of the food they provided.

Moreover, the lad astonished them by what he knew. He seemed able to identify every bird along the way, both by sight and song; and also nearly every kind of tree and wild plant. One afternoon, when they'd paused to relieve themselves, he spotted some wild mushrooms among the trees and began gathering them to add to their evening meal. "My grandfather taught me about these," he said. "They're called penny buns."

That same night, as they settled into their bedrolls, he rattled off the names of some of the stars and constellations that blanketed the sky above them; he pointed out Rigel in Orion—"one of the brightest of the fixed stars"— and then Mars and Venus—"those ones're known as moveable stars," he told them, " 'cuz they're always shifting about."

On the final evening of their journey, Colgrevaunce took the boy aside to have a private conversation. "Simon, do you know why we brought you with us?" the man asked.

"No, sir, no idea."

"Because we thought you were Lute's son."

"Me? You thought I was Matthew? Oh, sir, we're not at all alike. I do wish I was more like 'im."

"When you see the Prince Regent, we need you to be Lute's son. That's who he's expecting. If he discovers you aren't the Earl's son, it could be very bad for you. Do you understand?" Colgrevaunce didn't add that it could be very bad for himself as well.

"He's like ta hurt me?"

"It's a real possibility. So, mum's the word, eh?"

The boy rubbed his chin, trying to take in what the man was telling him. Finally he said, "I'll do my best not to let the cat out of the bag."

"Good. That's the idea."

The naïve little boy didn't know if he should be afraid or pleased. The idea that he might be Mathew amused him. The two of them were as different as chalk and cheese, as his grandfather might say.

As the group of riders descended the high hill across from

the city, the westering sun flamed in the sky creating orange and pink streaks.

"Day after tomorrow is All-Hallows Eve," Simon remarked to himself. "I wonder how them city folks celebrate it."

The little cavalcade began moving up the road that twisted through the water meadows, then neared the broad river.

"A drawbridge!" the boy squealed with delight. "Never seen one before. Is that the barbican?" he asked, pointing.

"The *what?*" one man said.

"It is," another one replied.

The wide-eyed boy entered the city gazing and gaping. "It's all so wonderful," he exclaimed.

"He might not think it's so wonderful tomorrow," one man muttered.

"Nah, the Prince ain't gonna hurt 'im," another man said. "I won't allow it."

"Har, har."

They passed upward through the successive levels of the city, eventually reaching the entrance to the castle. The men were happy to leave their horses in the capable hands of the stable boys and head off to their own chambers in the castle. Colgrevaunce led Simon straight on up to the quarters of Mordred, the Prince Regent.

Osmond, Mordred's chamberlain, opened the door and motioned for the boy to enter. The boy stepped anxiously into the regal apartment, and that was the last Colgrevaunce saw of him.

❖

It took Tom just two days to return to the city. Once more, he left his mount at his friend's farm outside the city. Since the horse wasn't Raguel and since this time Tom paid the fellow in advance, the man was less grumpy about it.

Now Tom sat in the warm kitchen at the back of the chandler's shop, eating a steaming bowl of chicken soup. Mary watched him affectionately as he soaked up the soup broth with a crust of bread.

"This little boy they've brought here," she asked, "who is he?" Gossip and rumors tended to spread quickly in the city, and many folks had watched with keen interest as Colgrevaunce and his troupe had escorted the boy up to the castle.

"Well, Mary, I can tell you who he *isn't*. He isn't who the Regent thinks he is."

"What do you think's likely to happen to 'im?"

Tom slurped down another spoonful of soup before replying. "Dunno, Mary. Ya think you 'n' Mags could maybe rescue the little fella?" When the expected look of fright spread across her face, Tom grinned. "Just joshin' ya, girl. If anyone's gonna rescue the lad, it's like ta be me."

They sat there for a few more minutes in companionable silence while Tom finished his simple meal. Then Mary scooped up the bowl and spoon, tidied up the table, and swept the last few breadcrumbs into her hand. "You have yourself a good rest tonight, Tom. We can be worrying about the little lad in the morning." Tom nodded, then stretched and yawned.

"You plannin' ta go to the minster tomorrow night?" he asked.

"Oh, aye. Those of us not on duty're expected ta be there."

"Mind if I go with ya?"

"Do ya think that would be safe?"

"Mary, once this little street urchin"—Tom pointed his finger at his own chest—"is all dressed up in his finery, no one's like ta recognize the little jackanapes." Tom grinned. Mary did, too. Then she leaned over and placed a kiss on his brow.

"You're *my* little jackanapes," she said.

Mordred sat and studied the young lad who stood still as a stone just inside the doorway to the Prince Regent's private sitting room. He could see nothing of Lute in the lumpy, pasty-faced boy. That surprised him.

"Come in, come in. Come over here and set yourself down close to the window. Let's have us a good visit, hm?"

The boy hesitated, then shuffled across the room to the chair at which Mordred had pointed. His face reflected various emotions—anxiety, excitement, curiosity, and fear among them. He needed to remember that he was supposed to be a nobleman's son, not a plain as dirt commoner, a tenant farmer's grandson. It wouldn't be easy.

"Your name is . . . *Simon?*"

"Yes sir, it is," the boy replied softly.

"Tell me, Simon, how is your father?"

"My *father?*" The boy sounded surprised by the question. "Sir, I hain't seen my father in a long, long time."

"Not for a few weeks, anyway," Mordred replied. "I guess to a boy that can seem like a long time."

"Oh, sir, it's been *much* longer'n that."

"Yes, well, all right then. Tell me, Simon, how do you like the city so far?"

"It's truly grand, sir. I'm very eager to learn all about it."

"Tomorrow evening you must accompany me to the minster. There we will attend the All-Hallows Eve service together. Would you like that?"

"I'd love it, sir. I never been to any minster before. Is it a kind of church?"

"Is it a kind of church? Oh, yes, Simon, it's a very big and splendid church."

"That's wonderful," the boy declared, his round face suffused with joy.

Mordred was finding it hard not to be charmed by the childish wonderment of this naive little fellow. Mordred hadn't brought the boy to the city to harm him, at least not right away. For now, he wanted him for leverage, or possibly even as bait. Of course, assuming it was true that Uther Pendragon's blood flowed through his veins, the lad would have to be killed eventually. But as Mordred studied the boy, he could see no obvious, outward sign of Pendragon blood. He looked rather like a pale and round-faced pudding. Mordred smiled at the thought. Perhaps the lad had the makings of a priest or a scholar but *never* a knight, let alone a king. No true Pendragon, Mordred thought, had the makings of a priest! Suddenly Mordred found his gorge rising. This little slug was an insult to his lineage—which was just one more reason to justify snuffing him out.

Mordred sighed. Well, snuffing the little fellow out wouldn't be any more momentous than squashing a bug. Even if the lad was turning out to be a rather likeable bug.

CHAPTER 15

As she did every morning when it wasn't raining, Margause, Mordred's mother, walked in one of the castle's main gardens, a heavy woolen cloak about her shoulders. She turned her head to the left and gazed at the splendid palace connected to the citadel by the high walkway. Since the queen's hasty flight to London a couple of weeks earlier, the palace had been essentially empty. That would change after Mordred's coronation at Christmas. Then she and the new king, along with their attendants, would shift their quarters from the castle over to the palace. Margause wished she could do that now, but she knew it wouldn't be seemly. Anyway, it would happen soon enough, and it would give her great pleasure to finally be installed there—after *much* too long a wait.

Many years earlier, after the death of King Uther, there had been a very good likelihood that Margause's husband, King Lot of Lothian, would become the next High King— since Uther had no known heirs and King Lot was one of the most prominent and accomplished of the lesser kings. Had that happened, Margause would have been living in the palace all this time. How she had wanted that to come about. But it hadn't. Almost as if out of nowhere, a son for Uther had suddenly emerged. Arthur, the previously unknown boy, had performed some stunning deeds to prove his right to the throne. It wasn't long before he'd won the hearts of the people. That whole miraculous business had probably been the work of Merlyn, Margause thought—that good-for-nothing old bastard!

Eventually, Margause had taken at least a partial revenge by seducing the young man and bearing his son, *Mordred*. And then, somehow, she'd managed to thwart that despicable attempt to kill all the little boys—at least in Mordred's case she'd thwarted it. She remembered the horrid little jingle that seemed to on everyone's lips at the time:

> *When a star falls on Beltaine Eve,*
> *So the Sybil once did say,*
> *A leopard born of a lion,*
> *Will Albion lead astray.*

Beltaine, the First of May, was precisely when Mordred was born, and there *had* been a starry portent the evening before. Margause never knew who was responsible for snatching her child from her—she suspected it had been Merlyn. But the ring she'd hung about the baby boy's neck like an amulet must've actually protected him. It was fifteen years before she saw him again. And he still had the ring!

The two of them, mother and son, were so alike in both looks and temperament, there could be little doubt that they were mother and son. Eventually, even Arthur came to acknowledge Mordred as his son. And then, when he departed on his ill-fated adventure across the water, almost two years ago, he'd appointed Mordred as Regent in his absence.

Nearly two years had now passed, and the King still hadn't returned. All the reports they'd received from abroad suggested that Arthur's endeavor had been a failure. It was now widely believed that the King must be dead. How fortuitous! In less than two months, Mordred would be the newly crowned king.

Once more Morgause gazed longingly at the palace. She believed it would soon be her home.

❖

"There's one spell you've never taught me," Nimuë said. She and Merlyn had been drinking elderflower tea and discussing potions and effusions. It was the second time he had allowed her to visit him in his special sanctum.

"A spell I haven't taught you? Which one would that be?" Merlyn replied, though he knew very well the one she had in mind.

"If you don't wish to teach it to me, Merlyn," she said coyly, "then I don't want to know it."

"Which one is it?" he asked again.

"Oh, never mind. It's not all that important."

Ha! Merlyn thought. It's *all* important.

Now Nimuë had moved to the back of the cave. She stood examining the shelves that held his various pots and jars, reading the labels on them.

"What's this one for?" she asked. "Atropa Belladonna."

"Oh dear, that one. In a small dose, it can be a very effective sleeping draught. In a larger dose, a very deadly poison. Great care must be used with that one."

"Now I remember," she said. "I've read about it in *Dioscorides's Herbal*."

"A dangerous book," Merlyn said.

"A delicious book," she replied. "Dangerous only to foolish or irresponsible users. And that's not us."

As Nimuë bent her head forward to read another label, a stray tendril of her dark hair slipped loose and fell in front of her ear brushing against her cheek. Merlyn felt a keen urge to reach out and tuck it back in place. He knew he daren't. While the desire was still in his mind, Nimuë lifted her hand and tucked her hair back behind her ear.

Chapter 16

I think we should take a shortcut," Lute said to Neely and Matty. "It'll mean a steep climb, but it will be worth it."

"Aha," Neely said, "goin' over Barham's Edge, eh? I remember it used to be one of your favorite places. You and Jill rode up there often."

"You *knew* that?"

" 'Course I did. Whole village knew it. People used to joke about it."

"Well, yes, Jill and I did ride up there together a few times," Lute said wistfully. "On top of Barham was where I made some important decisions."

The path they now followed took them up the steep slopes of a tree-clad escarpment. Soon the smell of the pinewoods filled their nostrils. Rags seemed to enjoy the challenge of the steep climb; Neely's horse was breathing hard before they reached the top.

Matthew's head twisted this way and that. There were astonishing views of the surrounding countryside in all four directions. "Golly," he said.

"Look down there to the west, Matt," Lute said. "See the wisps of smoke? That's where we're going. That's the little hamlet of Northering."

"Is that the place you consider home, Father?"

"I did once, but not anymore. Home is Sanham. Home is where I live with you and your mother and Editha."

"It's one of my two homes, Matty," Neely said. "Always good to have two. Somethin' happens ta one o' them, good ta have another un ta fall back on."

"That sounds like something Tom might say," Lute remarked.

"Oh no, father," Matthew said, "Tom told me he ain't never had no home."

"Lute!" boomed a deep male voice.

"Rob!" Lute shouted back. Lute leaped off of Raguel's back, and in a flash the two men were hugging. It had been three years since they'd last seen each other, but their friendship was so firm and deep that they could always pick up right where they left off. For the first sixteen years of their lives—until Lute, at Merlyn's insistence, had gone off to 'seek his fortune' in the city, the two of them hadn't spent a day apart. Lute had had no siblings—at that time he hadn't known about his half-brother, Mordred—and Rob was like a brother to him.

"Hello, Neely," Rob said. "And this is your little Matthew, eh Lute? He's grown tall since I last laid eyes on him."

"How ya doin', Rob?" Neely said. "You 'member that time you 'n' me scored the winning goal?"

"Neely's never forgotten his big moment," Lute said to Rob. "High point of his life."

"Nor have I forgotten it," Rob said. "Prettiest goal I ever saw. And I got an assist, too." Neely grinned, pleased by Rob's remark.

"Neely, could you and Matt take the horses and stable 'em? That be okay, Rob?" Rob nodded.

"Sure thing, Lute," Neely said. He and the boy led the horses away, giving Lute and Rob some privacy.

"So Lute, what's the occasion? The noble earl just had to come back and see how the simple folk were doing? Needed to give yourself a reminder of what real life is like?"

"I've never forgotten what real life is like, Rob. And you know I'm closer to being one of the simple folk, as you say, than I am to being one of the so-called nobles. And proud of it."

"Well, maybe," Rob said, still teasing.

"Rob, I have a huge favor to ask of you," Lute said.

"Ask away. If it's anything I can do, you know I won't hesitate."

"Would you take Matt under your wing for a while? Can't say for how long. And treat him like a member of your own family?"

Rob looked startled. "What's going on, Lute?"

"He's in danger, Rob."

"In danger? How so?"

"It's the Prince Regent. He's learned I have a son who's in the direct bloodline of Uther Pendragon. If I'm in danger, Rob—which I am—Matty is in the same danger. Maybe even more. As far as I know, they've never set eyes on him. But if he could stay with you, he'd blend in well with you and your own sons. It should be safe, since no one knows it was here that I grew up. Or that my own mother still lives here."

Rob rubbed one side of his face slowly, pondering Lute's words. "Lute, of course I will," he said at last. "The boys should get along well, I think. I'll just need to get Bridie to agree to it. I'll need to convince her that it poses no great danger to our family."

"It *does* pose some danger, Rob, I can't deny that."

"Well, I can," Rob said. "Lute, the lad will be safe with me." Lute reached out and griped his friend's shoulder and gave it a squeeze. Words weren't needed. Still, Lute was relieved at the reassurance.

"How's Jill?" Rob asked. "Well, I trust?" Rob had once been deeply enamored of Jill, though he'd always known it was Lute she preferred. And it had made more sense, Jill with Lute, both of them belonging to the noble class, while Rob was only a commoner. Neither Jill nor Lute had ever paid any attention to that supposed distinction, but Rob was always conscious of it.

"She's doing well, Rob. Jill's the same wonderful girl you and I grew up with. I doubt if she'll ever change."

"I've missed you two," Rob said. "Never been the same around here with you gone. I've had no one to give a hard time, Lute. Hey, here's an idea. Maybe you and Aldhelm could trade earldoms, and then you could come back here. Not that Aldhelm's not a pretty good fellow, for he is."

"Ha, ha, trade earldoms. Now, there's a notion!"

"Too bad it doesn't work that way," Rob said. "Well, I guess you'll want to go and see your mother. But soon, you must come and have a meal with us, and then we can kick things around with Bridget, eh? I'll go ahead and break the news to her in advance. I'm sure it will all work out. How do you think Matt will take to it?"

"He'll be delighted to have some 'brothers.' It will be just like it was for you and me, once upon a time."

"That pleases me, Lute. I think the boys will like it, too."

After Neely bid them goodbye and went off to his parents' house, Lute and Matthew began walking the half mile to Lute's mother's cottage.

"Matt, you remember Rob, don't you?" he asked his son.

"Yes, I do. And I remember Johnny, too. He was just my age. We got on really good."

"Would you mind staying with them for a while?"

Matt's disjointed thoughts suddenly came tumbling out. "Father, I know that a lot of strange things have been happening. Boy, what happened at Wat's cottage scared me pretty good. But our escape from those riders, golly, that was exciting. Raguel's an amazing horse. I bet he can outrun the North Wind. Father, do you think I might become a knight one day, just like you did?"

"Maybe so, Matt, if it's something you decide you truly want to do."

"I really hope so," the boy said a bit wistfully.

They walked on for another minute in silence.

Finally, Lute said, "You remember my mother, too,

don't you, Matt? I think you must've been about four the last time you saw her."

"Oh, yes, father. She's wonderful. How could I ever forget her?"

Lute couldn't help remembering a time when the King had said almost those same words to him—"She's wonderful. How could I ever forget her?" For Lute, it was a bittersweet memory. He knew that Arthur and his mother hadn't seen each other for more than the length of his lifetime, that they hadn't seen each other since a very few days after they had conceived him.

"Father, could I ask you something?"

"Of course, Matt."

"I will be very glad to see my grandmother. But Father, where is my grand*father*? Why has he never been there? Is he no longer living, like my other grandparents? He would be your father, wouldn't he?"

Lute wasn't sure what to say. "Yes, he would be my father, Matt," he finally managed.

"Father, back at Wat's cottage, Tom rode off on Swifty wearing my cloak. He was making those men think he was me. So those men must've been looking for me, right? Why were they? Was it because of your father, my grandfather?"

Lute stopped walking and stood still in the middle of the lane. Then he pulled the boy to him and held him in a firm embrace. "Matt, there's a great deal you've never been told. Things I thought it better to keep from you for a time. It appears that time is over. Yes, they *were* looking for you, Matt. And yes, they were looking for you because of who your grandfather is; and also because of who *his* father was. And they were also looking for you because of who I am. But most especially, Matt, they were looking for you because of who you are."

The boy stood still and stared. "Because of who *I* am?" he asked.

"Yes, Matthew, because of who you are."

Chapter 17

The minster's nave had begun filling an hour before the midnight service. Among the first to come were the families of the merchants and the lesser nobles; they sought seats as close to the rood screen as they could get. The vergers kept the central aisle clear so that the higher nobles, who would come later, could process down to the pews reserved for them in front of the chancel arch.

Tom and Mary also slipped in early and found a place for themselves on a low stone bench near the back of the nave just inside the North Porch. People weren't likely to take much notice of the nondescript little couple seated there in the dark corner, but it was a spot from which they could have a good view of the entire proceedings.

The candles in the wall sconces only illuminated the lower portions of the vast structure. The slender, elegant piers in the nave disappeared high above them in the gloom of the ceiling's rib vaulting. The choir stalls behind the roodscreen, which would soon be filled with brown-robbed monks, were more brightly lit by a great profusion of candles. The rose window, now dark, down at the farthest end of the apse could just be glimpsed by those in the nave through the open space beneath the cancel arch.

As the midnight hour approached, the highest-ranking

nobles began to arrive. "My word, Mary," Tom whispered, "it's Earl Thomas, Lute's uncle. Sure didn't expect ta see him." The elderly man moved slowly, a cherry-wood cane in his right hand, the woman on his left side helping to support him. "That's Juliana," Tom said. "She's one o' the kindest people I ever knew. She takes real good care o' the old fella."

The couple walked slowly all the way to the front row of pews. They then moved down the row to the far left end, nearly to the north transept, and took seats where the verger directed them.

As the assembled folks awaited the arrival of the Prince Regent and his entourage, two other figures came through the minster's great west door and began proceeding up the central aisle. They made a strikingly handsome pair. The man was Sir Pelleas, a well-known and much-admired young knight who had been one of the absent King's most trusted advisors. He was the youngest of Arthur's close friends, and one of the few who still remained in the city, since Sir Kay and Sir Bedivere accompanied the Queen in her hasty flight to London. The young woman with him was unknown to everyone present. She wore a flowing burgundy gown that could just be glimpsed beneath her black cloak. The hood of her cloak was thrown back to display her lovely face, which was framed by long, dark, wavy tresses. Murmurs of surprise and wonderment swept through the nave at the sight of the couple.

"Who's that with Sir Pelleas, Tom?" came Mary's whispered question.

"Don't know for sure. I've a notion, though."

"Well, tell me."

"Just might be that she's a friend of Merlyn's, my girl. That's just a hunch."

"Of Merlyn's! Well, I'll be."

Next Queen Margause entered, escorted by the Duke of Ortwick, a gaunt, string bean of a man, who was also one of her son's most avid advisors and supporters. The Duke had long despised the King. At one time he had been a protégé of King Lot of Lothian, Margause's now-deceased husband. But when Lot didn't become king, the fellow's fortunes had plummeted. More recently, with Mordred as the Prince Regent, his fortunes were on the upswing.

"A dangerous man, that," Tom murmured. "Fella knows me, too. Don't want him catchin' sight o' me."

"Goodness, Tom, maybe we'd best slip away."

"No, no. Not till the service is over."

Of course the service couldn't begin until the Prince Regent finally made his entrance. When he did, to the amazement of most of the folks there, he was accompanied by a small boy. As was his wont, Mordred was entirely dressed in black—black doublet, black tabard, black silk stockings—while the boy who walked at his side was garbed in a long black velvet cloak. The lad was so short that the cloak brushed the flagstones of the floor as he moved along.

Few people there had any idea who the boy might be, even though rumors about the boy Sir Colgrevaunce had brought had swept through the city. Tom was one of the few who actually knew something about the lad.

"Oh, Goodness, Tom," Mary whispered. "What do you make of this?"

"The man's a devious bastard, Mary, that's what I make of it. Up to some sort of devilry, like as not."

"Think you can do something about it?"

"Might be able to. Best to wait and see, though."

"Oh, the poor little fella," she murmured.

After just another brief moment, the monks began to enter. Chanting a plain song in unison, they filed slowly into the choir stalls. When they were settled there, the bishop stepped to the lectern. With upraised arms he began reciting scripture: "*Foli charissimi—ambulate in diletione et Christus dilexit nos*—Dear children, walk in love, also as Christ hath loved us. Let's us pray."

Everyone dropped down upon their knees while the bishop intoned a short invocation. At the end of it, the voices of all the people united, "Amen."

The All-Hallows Eve service was underway.

❖

The fire flared in the grate and a coal slipped out onto the hearth. Matt was on it in a flash. He scooped it up with the small shovel and slid it back amongst the glowing embers in the fireplace. The small room was illuminated only by the fire, but Lute, his mother, and Matthew didn't feel a need for additional light. It was warm and cozy inside the small cottage. Matt would soon be climbing up to the loft and the small bed there, but he was in no hurry. He enjoyed listening to the shared remembrances of his father and grandmother. It was here in this little cottage, in this little hamlet called Northering, where his father had lived for the first sixteen years of his life, a period in his father's life Matt knew little about.

His grandmother spoke softly of the project she was working on, a grand tapestry commissioned by the local earl, a man named Aldhelm. Aldhelm wanted it to be a hunting scene, and she'd decided she would make it a boar hunt. Leonore had created a forest setting teeming with hunting dogs, some on leashes, some ranging freely about the cornered the prey. The huntsmen were on foot, several of them holding their spears at the ready, a few sounding their hunting horns. Near them, on horseback, rode a pair of nobles, a man and a woman.

"Matt," she said, "I modeled the riders on your mother and father." Her comment brought a smile to Lute's face.

Lute found the detail she'd achieved, in both the dress of the people and the realistic depiction of the forest, quite astonishing. As a boy he'd always loved the complex designs and colorful patterns of his mother's creations. In their dining room at Sanham, one of them now hung proudly. But the realism of this scene she was creating seemed to him to be quite a departure from what he'd known her do before.

"I wonder what the boar feels like, being cornered like that," the boy said.

"I had wondered just that very thing as I was making him," his grandmother replied. "I wanted his face to show both fear and determination. Boars are fierce and brave creatures, I believe. It's quite a challenge to hunt them. Quite dangerous, too."

"Have you hunted a boar, Father?"

"Only once. And I have to admit I felt sorry for the noble creature."

"Your father has always had a tender heart," she said.

"Yes, grandmother. And maybe I have inherited one from him."

"Well," she replied, "that wouldn't be such a bad thing, Matthew."

Chapter 18

It took Lute a day and a half to reach Merlyn's cave. He didn't know the best route to follow, but Raguel did, so Lute simply gave the horse his head. As the horse and rider moved up the Wye Valley, mist enshrouded the tops of the surrounding hills. November had come.

Lute and Raguel drew to a halt as close to the entrance as they could get. They heard a loud voice sounding from behind the invisible barrier: "I thought I told you *not* to ride that accursed creature! Well, I guess the horse is already out of the barn, so to speak."

"Good morning, Merlyn. Got up on the wrong side of bed?"

"Bed? What bed? No bed in here that I can see."

"It's an expression, sir."

"So it is. Anyway, sorry to have snapped at you, lad. So why don't we start over?"

"Good morning, sir," Lute called out. "How are you this fine day?"

"Just a bit grumpy, Lute, I have to confess it." Raguel snorted. "And I don't need any wisecracks from you, horse," Merlyn snapped. "Did you get there in time to save the boy?"

"He's safe so far, sir. Mostly Tom's doing. He's with

my friend Rob in Northering, and I feel pretty optimistic about it."

"That's us, isn't it, one grumpy, one optimistic."

"I hurried back here, sir, because of the other thing you said when we were here earlier. You said that after getting Matty to safety, I must try and help the King. So, please, sir, please explain to me what you meant by that, if you've a mind to tell me."

"Lute, they're trying to keep him from coming back. They mean to *finish* him."

"They?"

"Mordred and his band of Myrmidons, of course," Merlyn said snappishly. "Who else would it be?"

Lute was silent for a moment before saying, "What must I do?"

"You must find Sir Pelleas and Nimuë. Pelleas must then gather up everyone he knows in the court who is still loyal to the King. There may not be so many of you. Then, fast as you can, you must assemble a force and go to Milford Haven. That's where your father and his fleet will be making their landing. Arthur thinks that's far enough out of the way that Mordred will be none the wiser. He's wrong. Mordred is aware of his plans, and he and his troops will be there waiting as he disembarks. They intend to destroy him and what remains of his army, once and for all."

"Sir, no disrespect, but how do you know all of this?"

"Oh . . . well . . . there are ways for someone like me to know such things. Unfortunately, there's also a price to be paid for the knowing. Let's just leave it at that, eh?"

"Sir, I don't know Sir Pelleas or Nimuë. I've never met them. Where can I find them?"

"They're in the city. Tom will know. I doubt if he's met Nimuë, but he'll still know how to find them. Little Tom is no Tom Fool." Merlyn chuckled, remembering when the little lad first explained to him how he'd come to choose his own name.

"Who is this Nimuë?" Lute asked. "I've never heard of him."

"*Her*, Lute, Nimuë's a her, not a him." Oh, yes, he thought to himself, she's definitely a *her*.

"A *her*?" Lute said. "Well, all right, then, but why is she important? What can she do to help the King?"

"Ah, what *can't* she do? Lute, she knows everything I know. She can do anything that I might be able to do. And fortunately, she's not quite as tainted as I am."

"*Tainted*? I don't understand."

"No, you don't. Just take my word for it, eh? Lute, go and find Tom in the city. After that, you will have to figure things out as best you can."

Lute expelled a deep breath. "Well, sir, a man can but essay. Oh, and what shall I do about Rags?"

"Have you any money?"

"Some."

"Leave him with Tom's friend. You know the one I mean, just outside the city. Pay the fellow up front. I'll send him a dream tonight to encourage him a little, just to be on the safe side."

"You can send people dreams?"

"Of course not, Lute. I was only joshing. What do you think I am, anyway?"

"Perhaps I'd better not say," Lute replied. Instead of snorting, Raguel broke wind.

❖

Brogan felt at loose ends. At the Earl of Sanham's manorial compound, everything was calm and quiet. Lute and Matthew were gone. Tom and Neely were gone. Even the boy Simon was gone, whisked away by Colgrevaunce and his ruffians. After the thrilling days he'd experienced in the city, life here at the manor had become exceedingly boring. Some bad blood seemed to have developed between Eldred and Willykin, but who knew what that was all about. Some little personal matter, no doubt.

Brogan's thoughts kept returning to the city. The events that had occurred during his few days there had been anything but boring. For a country fellow like him, they'd been exhilarating. He'd been imprisoned in the great citadel, including a cell deep in its donjon, and then he'd been thrust into the castle's great hall in full view of all the great nobles, where he'd even exchanged words with the Prince Regent. Apparently, he'd impressed the fellow! But amongst all the people he'd encountered there, there was one in particular who was etched very firmly in his mind—a tall woman with a generous heart. He'd only seen her four or five times, but to Brogan she was unforgettable. Magdalene, that was her name! He wondered if she still remembered him. Probably not, he thought. Why in the world would she?

But stalwart fellow that he was, he wouldn't heed the siren call to return to the city. He would stay put and make sure the Lady Jillian and her daughter Editha were as secure as he could make them. He had his responsibilities at the manor, overseeing things in the Earl's absence. He wasn't one to shirk them. His first loyalties weren't to himself, they were to Lute and to the Lady Jillian.

❖

As Lute walked the mile and a half from the farmstead where he'd left Raguel, he saw that a great wall of thick mist was moving in from the west. The city would soon be enveloped in it, a fact that suited Lute's purposes well. He didn't know how to contact Tom, whom he assumed was now in the city, and he knew virtually nothing about Sir Pelleas and Nimuë. So his immediate plan was to slip secretly into his uncle's demesne and see what Earl Thomas might be able to tell him. His uncle's house, he knew, was probably being watched. But this sea of misty fog would give him cover as he moved through the city.

By the time he'd passed through the city's great gateway, dense fog obscured most of the structures in the lowest of the city squares. Lute could make out the gray moving shapes of only a few people. The central fountain was now practically invisible. Through the moist air orange-ish lights emanated from the flambeaux and the iron cressets that flared and glowed outside the entrances to the city's public houses. But even the sounds coming from within them seemed muted by the thick, dank atmosphere.

Eschewing the central stairs that ascended to the city's upper levels, Luke selected a particularly dark alleyway he remembered that led upward not far from the city's encircling wall. As he navigated the fog-enshrouded lanes he saw no one, and in less than ten minutes he was creeping into the shadowy darkness of the narrow alley that ran behind his uncle's back garden. He slipped cautiously along the high wall until he reached a spot where he knew he could hoist himself over. He broke into a dash to build up momentum and then, placing his hands atop the six-foot high stone wall, he vaulted over it. Lute landed inside on the grassy verge bordering Gwilym's favorite bed of roses. Fortunately, the roses had been spared, and Lute breathed a sigh of relief, knowing he would be spared the wrath of Gwilym.

But it wasn't Gwilym who answered Lute's tap on the kitchen door. "Lute!" Juliana cried, flinging her arms about him. "Your uncle and I were just wondering about you. And now, here you are."

"Speak of the devil," Earl Thomas said grinning, once Juliana had led him through several passages and shepherded him into the toasty sitting room where a fire crackled in the iron grate. A marmalade cat lay dozing on the hearth. "Sit, lad, sit," Thomas said, pointing to the empty chair to his left.

"You look well, Uncle," Lute said, smiling warmly. "I'm delighted to see that." He gave his uncle's left forearm an affectionate squeeze before seating himself.

"The *boy*, Lute," Earl Thomas suddenly expostulated, "who is he? I know that he can't be your son Matthew."

"The boy? Sir, what boy are you speaking of?"

"The one with Mordred. The one Colgrevaunce brought here a few days ago. The one so many folks in the city have been nattering about. Do you have any idea who he could be?"

"Colgrevaunce brought the Prince Regent a boy? Goodness, that's strange. And you're right that he can't be my Matthew. Matthew's been tucked safely in a place far, far away. Sir, can you describe this boy?"

"He's probably about eight or nine years old," Earl Thomas said. "He's short, a bit chubby, with a round, pasty-looking face. He seems to be a bit shy, but to all appearances, a dutiful little fellow."

"My word, Uncle. The lad you're describing sounds a lot like Simon, Wat's grandson."

"Wat's grandson? Why on earth would they bring him here?"

"That's a very good question. But Uncle, they did come to the manor seeking Matthew. Fortunately, we got him away in the nick of time. It doesn't seem likely they could've mistaken Simon for Matthew, but maybe they did. Or maybe there's some devilry going on that I don't understand."

"Lute, I'll see what more I can find out about the lad. I still have a friend or two in the castle."

"Speaking of friends, Merlin told me that I should seek out a knight called Sir Pelleas. He's someone I know nothing about."

"Sir Pelleas. Yes, that makes sense. He arrived at court maybe a year or so after your sudden and mysterious departure, Lute. That might be nine or so years back. He's a very able fellow. He quickly proved his knightly prowess and established himself as a man of true integrity. Arthur came to value him greatly, and I know he trusts him implicitly. It wouldn't surprise you, then, to hear that Sir Pelleas is no favorite of Mordred. Actually, if truth be told, I think Mordred may fear him."

"And what of Nimuë, sir? What do you know of her?"

"Ah. Now that's a tougher one. She's a woman around whom there's a good bit of mystery. It was Sir Palomides who first brought her to court a few weeks ago. The poor fellow was completely smitten by her—no surprise there, given his amorous proclivities and her great beauty—but the woman soon showed she had no use for him and avoided him. She has presented herself very favorably, though, and has become friendly with the small group of knights still loyal to the King—especially Sir Pelleas. Rumor has it that she had had some sort of involvement with Merlyn. Anyway, she and Sir Pelleas seem to have become, umm, quite close friends."

"Aha. Involvement with Merlyn. Well, all of that does make a little bit of sense to me. You mentioned the King still having a small group of loyal supporters. Are there many of them?"

"Hard to say. Folks loyal to the King tend to keep quiet about that. Not a good idea to risk alienating the Prince

Regent or any of those loyal to him. The Prince Regent is top dog right now, and wise folk heed that fact. But Lute, you do realize how much danger you are in yourself, don't you?"

"I do, sir, but it's the King I care about. Merlyn firmly believes he's alive and that he's returning. He says it's up to us to help him. That's why I must find Sir Pelleas. Together we might be able to provide the King some aid."

"Together you might. It won't be easy, but together the two of you might."

"Three of us, sir—there's Nimuë, too."

As Merlyn looked out through the cave's opening—out through his invisible prison door—his thoughts reverted to Nimuë and his final meeting with her. It was a memory tinged with sadness.

She had appeared unexpectedly late one afternoon. It had been several weeks since he'd last seen her, and he'd begun to think she might never return—though he knew deep down she *had* to return—in order to extract from him that one final, essential bit of information she so much desired.

Her face was paler than usual, her dark hair pulled back and twisted into a single braid that hung down her back. Her slender, alabaster neck was fully displayed. Merlyn had never desired her so greatly.

She offered him a sly, subtle smile, knowing that on this visit there would be nothing he could deny her. He was hers to bend, twist, mold in any way she chose.

Merlin studied her as she stood silently at the entrance to his hillside chamber. The late afternoon sun was just dipping behind the edge of the high mountain shoulder visible behind her.

Finally Merlyn spoke. "So, you've come at last." Nimuë gave a barely perceptible nod. "Well, then," he said, "we'd best set about finishing things between us. Yes?"

"Yes," she replied softly, still nodding slightly. "It's time we did."

Neither of them spoke for a long moment.

"It's the spell you'll be wanting. Yes?" Merlyn said.

Again she nodded.

"And you do know there is a price?" he said, with a grim smile.

"There is *no* price," she said.

"No price that you aren't willing to pay?" he asked.

"No. There isn't any price that I must pay. You must give it to me willingly. If you won't, then I don't want it. But if you give me the spell, we might consider what would be a most fitting recompence."

"You know, Nimuë," Merlyn said with a very tight smile, "I don't trust you for one single second. But I also know, as do you, there is nothing I can deny you."

"Well, sir, I am waiting."

Merlyn breathed a deep, deep sigh. "As I have been," he said, "for a very great while. All right, then, listen closely. I am only going to tell you just the one time."

Nimuë did listen closely as the old man spoke slowly and distinctly, his words becoming firmly etched in her brain. When he'd finished, he looked more exhausted than ever.

She reached out and touched his hand. "Thank you," she said. "You've always said that the one person you care most about in the world is the King. You have just done what you never wanted to do; but in the process, you have done what you very much wanted to do."

"Are you speaking in riddles?" he said. "Well, you haven't baffled me. But you do know, Nimuë, that there is one last thing I very, very much wish to do."

"And that, sir, is something that you shall never do."

Before she departed, Nimuë did do one final thing herself. It wasn't what the lusty old man had fervently hoped for. And yet it was something he'd known all along was inevitable—for she left him there all alone. And alone he would be, shut up inside his private abode, until the end of his days.

Merlyn had long known what his final fate would be, and he was reconciled to it—at least, as reconciled as one could be. It was the price he had to pay. It was recompense for all his misdeeds. Merlyn felt sorry for some of those misdeeds—but if truth be told, not all that sorry.

❖

Tom was lying low. He occupied his daylight hours performing needed tasks for Mary's father back in the workroom section of the chandler's shop. He prepared rush wicks for the cheaper candles and the rush lights; he heated up various mixtures of tallow, wax, and grease for the different varieties of candles and tapers; he scraped and cleaned the candle molds. His skillful hands did much to ingratiate him to Mary's father.

At supper each evening he teased out of Mary, and Magdalene whenever she joined them, what information he could about the doings up at the castle. The pair of women knew the kinds of information he wanted and were always attentive to that. The most recent thing they'd told him was that Simon was now studying a few hours each afternoon with Father Urias, the novice-master at the minster. The monk was working with the lad, along with all his other charges, on their reading and writing and on their study of the Holy Scriptures. Tom was acquainted with Father Urias. Perhaps he could make good use of this wise and honest monk.

"That tall fellow," Magdalene said to Tom, "the man who remained behind when you helped the other two to escape, what can you tell me about him?" She was referring to Brogan.

"Not much," Tom replied, "'cuz I don't really know 'im. But Lute believes in 'im, and that's good enough for me. Brave thing he done, givin' hisself up so's the others could get away, eh?"

"Where do you suppose he is now?"

"*That* I do know. He's back at the manor house in Sanham, a-doin' his job."

"Mags took quite a liking to that fella, don't ya know," Mary said, grinning at her friend. "And her always turnin' a blind eye to men's advances, too. Maybe not so much in this fella's case."

"He made no advances," Magdalene replied, blushing. "I only seen him maybe three or four times, and we hardly exchanged a word."

"When it comes ta pickin' out a stout fella," Tom said, "you could hardly do better."

Mary reached out and patted Magdalene on the forearm. "My Tom always knows what he's talkin' about," she said.

"I was just wonderin' about him is all," Magdalene said, still blushing.

Chapter 19

Simon," Mordred said, "would you like to learn about fencing?"

"Fencing? You mean with swords and rapiers and things like that?"

"Yes, Simon, that's what I mean. To be a knight, you must become an expert fencer."

"I like learning new things, so yes, I would like to learn about fencing."

"Then come along with me this morning. Perhaps it will be something you'll take to."

Three mornings a week Mordred engaged in fencing practice. He took pride in his skills and kept them as sharp as possible. From early in his teens, he'd been able to best nearly everyone, even seasoned and highly skilled knights. His sole public defeat had come at the hands of Sir Lamorak, when Mordred was just a fledgling trainee. It was a defeat he never forgot—or forgave.

Fascinated, Simon watched as the fit young athletes donned their fencing gear. He watched as they stretched out their limbs in preparation for their practice bouts; and once they'd begun, he watched them with awe as their blades flashed and slashed, as they parried and riposted, feinted and lunged. He listened to the men's grunts and curses and the sounds of their lightweight boots on the flagstone floor. Good footwork, the boy quickly perceived, was vital to a fighter's success.

Mordred, Simon saw, was light on his feet and possessed the limber, muscular legs of a dancer. His lightning-quick movements showed agility and grace. Simon couldn't help admiring the man's athleticism. But when Mordred suddenly lunged at his opponent, flicking the blade's tip toward his opponent's throat with his slender arm and agile wrist, it had the look of a snake suddenly striking its prey. Simon shivered at the sight.

Simon decided he liked the flash and dash of fencing. But, realizing that the sport's goal was to injure or even kill one's opponent, he concluded that fencing really wasn't something he wanted any part of himself.

Most people at the castle treated Simon quite kindly and were eager to accommodate the likeable little chap. Amused by how the lad loved to eat, folks readily provided him with sumptuous, delicious meals. But after a few days of eating the refined delicacies of a nobleman, Simon found himself missing the simple fare he'd eaten at his grandfather's farm. And even more, he really missed his grandfather. The truth was, Simon was lonely.

He did, however, make one friend, the young Squire named Yonec, who was assigned the duty of being the boy's attendant. The two of them enjoyed exploring the citadel complex together, a duty Yonec didn't seem to find demeaning. Together they wandered through the castle's many hallways, walkways and public spaces, including the castle's several chapels, the great hall, the kitchens, and the solars. As they did, Yonec explained the functions of the various rooms and structures, and Simon's active young brain absorbed it all avidly. The curious little boy always had many questions for Yonec—questions the young squire *usually* could answer.

Each afternoon Yonec accompanied Simon down to the great minster on the city's second level. There, in a well-lit corner of the cloisters, along with the young novices who were preparing for holy orders, the boy received instruction from Father Urias, the novice-master. Under Father Urias's watchful eye, the boy had his first experiences of books. To Simon, they were more wondrous than anything he had ever encountered—including all the wonders at the castle.

On the morning of November 11—it was Saint Martin's Day—Yonec led Simon up the steep steps of the citadel's second tallest tower, the tallest being off-limits to all but the most exalted nobles. From where they stood, the boy could look out over the city and even much of the surrounding countryside. During the night the city had been shrouded in a thick fog, but it was gone now, and the city seemed aglow in the morning's bright sunshine.

Simon gazed down in awe on King Uther Pendragon's crowning achievement. He ran his eyes over the rooftops of the city's many diverse structures, smoke rising from chimneys of the houses and shops; he took in the sight of the soaring spires of the city's numerous churches; he slowly traced the great central staircase as it descended down through the successive levels of the city. Pausing on each level, he admired the squares and fountains that graced each one. He examined the high, crenelated walls that encircled the city, their guard towers spaced along them at regular intervals. Lastly, the boy gazed out upon the fields and meadows that spread out across the countryside beyond the city walls. Somewhere out there, several days ride beyond those fields, lay his grandfather's little farmstead. When would he see it again?

Simon's thoughts were interrupted by the sound of footsteps ascending the stairs. A moment later the head and then the upper body of a man appeared. "Good morning," the man said. "Wonderful day to enjoy the view. Do you mind if I join you?"

"No, not at all . . . oh . . . , Sir Pelleas!" Yonec stammered with surprise. He quickly dipped his head as a sign of respect for the celebrated knight.

"You are Yonec, I believe," the man said. "But this young fellow is someone I don't know."

"This is Simon," Yonec replied. "He's the guest of the Prince Regent. I've been giving him a tour of the castle."

"Simon, I'm delighted to make your acquaintance. You are new to the city?" The shy boy nodded. "And what's your opinion of our city so far? It must all seem quite strange and new to you."

"It's not like anything I have ever seen, not like

anything I ever even imagined, sir. It . . . it's . . . ."

"Yes, leaves you rather speechless? It did me when I first saw it. Designed by King Arthur's father. King Uther had some splendid architects and engineers, and they picked the perfect place to build a totally new city. Built it from the ground up. And all in a decade, no mean achievement."

"Sir," Simon said, "I don't reckon you knew King Uther. But do you know King Arthur?"

"Yes, old Uther was a good bit before my time, so I didn't know him. But I do know the King. He's a man I much admire."

"Sir, if you'll pardon me for asking, where is he? Why isn't he here? Shouldn't he be here, overseeing things in his father's fine city?"

"Yes," Sir Pelleas mused, "a very good question— where is he? Simon, I don't actually know. He had some terribly pressing business that required him to go far away. Perhaps he'll soon return. Some of us hope so." Simon noticed that Sir Pelleas and Yonec exchanged knowing looks. He wasn't sure what that meant.

"And if he doesn't return, then the Prince Regent will become king?"

"Yes, Simon," Sir Pelleas said, "that's right." He looked grim as he made that admission. Simon could tell that for this man, it wasn't a happy thought.

❖

In addition to being blessed with great curiosity, Simon was also blessed with acute hearing. And one evening toward mid-November, as he was lying in his little bed trying to drop off to sleep, he heard the sound of muffled voices coming from the adjoining room. Simon's small chamber, which was hardly more than a closet, was separated from Mordred's spacious sitting room by a thick stonewall and a massive oaken door. The boy discovered that when he placed his ear up against the crack where the door's edge snugged against the jamb, he could just make out the men's voices in the next room.

Mordred's voice he recognized easily. The others he wasn't so sure of. One of them sounded like Colgrevaunce. There were maybe half a dozen voices in all. It took a while for the lad to get any sense of what was being discussed, though it was obvious from Mordred's tone of voice that he was upset. Apparently, something in the Prince Regent's plans had gone awry.

"My liege," a man declared, "you can't do anything about the weather. That's in God's hands. There's tricky winds out there on those treacherous waters."

"So the truth is, we have no bloody idea where they may end up?" asked Mordred.

"If we're lucky," another man said, "they'll end up at the bottom of the sea."

"A real possibility," said yet another speaker, "but we have to know."

"We have scouts everywhere," the first speaker said. "Sire, we have them all along the south coast from Land's End to St. David's. We'll know within days if and when they make landfall and where—and maybe they never will."

"Within days," Mordred scoffed. "And how many additional days will it take us to re-deploy our forces to wherever they are?"

"Sire, we'll do our best. That's all we can do."

"Sire, even if they manage to land safely, the King's army is weak and depleted. Ours is far superior. Once we have them cornered, we'll chew 'em to bits, like terriers on a pack of rats."

The room remained quiet for several seconds. Simon pressed his ear harder against the crack in the door. Finally Mordred said, "Yes, I know you'll do your best. We'll just have to play the hand we're dealt. The bloody weather. Well, let's hope we can put an end to this troublesome King, once and for all."

"Yes, sire, we must. And sire, we shall."

Although this overheard conversation hadn't made much sense to him, Simon tucked it away inside his young brain. He found the phrase "like terriers on a pack of rats" rather alarming. Although he'd never seen what terriers could do to rats, he could imagine it.

Juliana, wrapped in a heavy woolen shawl, sat on a bench near the central fountain in the midmorning sun. On this somewhat chilly November day the square was quiet and nearly empty. Holding her knitting in her lap, she kept a close eye on anyone who entered the square. Not many people did. She often came here to sit and knit, and today she'd come to the square in hopes of seeing one person in particular, Sir Pelleas. This morning, though, her hopes were in vain. He hadn't come.

She was about to gather her belongings and return home when she realized that someone was quickly descending the stairs from the city's highest level. It was a young woman with a long braid of black hair down her back. She looked vaguely familiar, but Juliana couldn't place her. To her surprise, the young woman, after briefly hesitating, approached her. She stood there for a long moment, studying the garment Juliana had been working on.

"That's lovely work you're doing," she said admiringly. "You are very skillful."

"Thank you," Juliana replied. "My mother taught me well. And in the years since then, I've had lots of practice."

"And the shawl you're wearing, is that your handiwork also?" Juliana nodded. "It's a beautiful pattern. So intricate. Is it of your own design?"

"Oh, no. It's quite an ancient design. I believe it comes originally from Scotia."

"Ah, Eriu, Hibernia."

Juliana laughed in surprise at the young woman's words. "You sound like a scholar. Are you, perchance?"

The young woman shrugged. "Maybe just a bit of one."

"Are you new to the city?" Juliana asked. "I don't believe I've seen you before."

"New as of three weeks ago. My name is Nimuë."

"And I'm Juliana."

"Juliana, if I were to come here again tomorrow, might

you show me how to make the kind of stitches you used on your shawl? If you could, I would be most grateful."

"Yes, I could do that. I come here most mornings, if it isn't too chilly or raining. Today it was *almost* too chilly."

"I shall bring my own yarn and needles," the younger woman said. "I certainly hope the weather cooperates."

"I won't mind," Juliana said, "if it's a trifle nippy. I'm made of fairly stern stuff.'

"Nor will I mind. It will be wonderful to make a new friend in the city. I know very few people here."

"Well, Nimuë, I shall look forward to seeing you tomorrow."

Nimuë remained there watching as Juliana strolled across the square. It was only a short walk to the front gate of the house she shared with Earl Thomas. And suddenly Nimuë caught movement out of the corner of her eye. Someone else was observing Juliana, a fellow lurking in back of the central fountain. Nimuë herself slipped behind the thick trunk of an elm and cautiously peeked around it. She watched the watcher. Why, she wondered, would someone be so very interested in keeping an eye on this innocent-seeming woman?

Lute felt stifled. He knew his uncle's home was being watched and that if he were to make a move, his presence was likely to be discovered. Juliana's contact with Nimuë, though, might be a promising start. Perhaps through her he could contact Sir Pelleas, as Merlin had advised. But if they alerted the wrong people, it could spell disaster to their cause.

In the early morning, a steady rain was falling. Then the skies cleared, and Juliana decided to go out to the bench in the square. Perhaps Nimuë would still come. She carefully stepped around the many puddles that had formed on the cobblestones. Someone was already waiting for her beside the bench where she normally sat, but it wasn't Nimuë.

The woman standing there was short and round-faced. Julianna didn't know her, but she had seen her before, making her way up to the citadel where she probably worked as a chambermaid or kitchen helper.

"Dame Juliana?" came the woman's soft voice.

"Yes, that's who I am."

"I've brought a message, m'lady. It's down back o' the bench leg, a small, folded bit o' parchment. Don't be pickin' it up just yet, not till I's long gone. A-fore ya do, be mighty sure no one's a-watchin'. There do be watchful eyes, this close to the castle."

"Yes, I'm afraid so."

"It's for Lute," the woman said. Juliana's eyebrows went up. "From Tom. Well, I'd best be off. I'll catch a good scolding if I'm late."

"Thank you," Juliana said to the back of the retreating figure. The small woman scurried toward the stairway leading up to the citadel. Then she ascended the steps swiftly.

❖

Mordred was thinking about the woman he'd seen with Sir Pelleas, the woman he now knew was called Nimuë. She was stunningly attractive, though he found it quite odd that he didn't desire her. She intrigued him, and indeed, while she caused him mild trepidation, she didn't arouse him—him, a man whose concupiscence was aroused by the sight of almost every lovely woman; a man who, as a young teenager, tumbled the local lasses in the bracken every chance he got; him, who as a knight-aspirant, had regularly enjoyed the favors of the ladies of the night down on the city's lowest level. The simple fact was that he'd lusted after the Queen, his father's wife, from the first time he'd seen her.

What did arouse him, though, was the thought of *killing* Nimuë. And something inside him told him he'd better do that soon. Nimuë, he felt certain, spelled trouble. He'd heard the rumor that she'd been Merlyn's mistress. That in itself placed her high on his most hated list, for Mordred despised anyone who had friendly associations with Merlyn—and that included his own father, King Arthur, and his own half-brother, Lute. Speaking of Lute, where was Lute? Why hadn't he reacted to the abducting of his son? Was it possible that Simon *wasn't* his son?

As Mordred was thinking about Lute and Simon, Osmond entered and said, "Your breakfast, sire. Shall I call the lad?"

"Umm," mumbled Mordred, nodding his head.

The boy, as usual, wasn't shy about eating. He was working on his third buttered scone when Mordred asked him an unexpected question. "Simon," he said, "do you know who I am?"

The boy pondered the question for a moment as he swallowed what was in his mouth. "Sir," he said, "you are the Prince Regent."

"And do you know what that is?"

"I know that at Christmas they plan to make you our new king."

"Ah, so you know that? Well, good. And do you know what kingship is, Simon?"

The boy was about to take another bite of scone, but he stayed his hand. "I think, sir, it means being over everyone else."

"Indeed. But it also involves how one should *act* while being over everyone else. It involves how a king should *behave*. Do you have any ideas about that?"

"No, sir, I don't. What would you say?"

"Well, let's talk about that. A learned writer I've read believes that the king should possess the qualities of the lion, the fox, and the pelican."

The boy tilted his head to one side, squinted his eyes, and puffed out his lower lip.

"He should be like the lion," Mordred went on, "because lions are strong, brave, and ferocious. He should be like the fox because the fox is cunning and quick thinking. And he should be like the pelican because pelicans are said to suckle their young on their own heart's blood. That means that they are compassionate and self-sacrificing, and they care for others more than for themselves. A king, the writer says, should be all those things."

Simon looked thoughtful. He tapped his lips with the

fingers of one hand. Finally he said, "O' course, I've never seen a lion, but I've heard they're brave and powerful. I *have* seen foxes, and I know, sir, how sly and tricky they can be. But pelicans? No, sir, I don't think so, sir. I do know a lot about birds. And I don't believe pelicans feed their young like that."

"No, you're probably right. But some books say so. Anyway, the idea is that a king should always take good care of his people."

Simon nodded his agreement. "Sir, I like that idea."

"I do, too," Mordred said. He said it, though he didn't mean it. Mordred had no doubt that he possessed the characteristics of the lion and fox. But he, like every true Pendragon, couldn't care less about the softer virtues. His father, Mordred knew, had been the one exception. That was a fact that disgusted him.

"Do you think your father would make a good king, Simon?" Mordred asked the boy.

Simon looked aghast. "*My* father? Oh no, sir, he would make a horrible king."

"Really? That bad?"

Suddenly it came to Simon that the Prince Regent might be asking him about Matthew's father, not his own. He recalled Sir Colgrevaunce warning him that he must pretend to be the son of the Earl, not that of an ignorant peasant farmer, like he truly was. He hoped he hadn't blundered, though maybe he had. Now he wasn't sure what to do.

"That bad. Eh?" Mordred said again. Now the boy just

shrugged.

"And what about you, Simon? Would you like to be king?"

"*Me?*" The boy was startled. "Oh no, sir, not a bit of it. I know I got no lion or fox in me, nor any pelican, either—no, not one tiny bit o' any o' them."

"No? Then what would you like to be?"

The boy paused for a moment giving the question some thought. "I surely do like Father Urias. Maybe I'd like ta be like him."

"Yes," said Mordred, a sneer forming on his lips, "maybe you would." This boy was a Pendragon? Never in life. Or in *death*, Mordred thought. But perhaps he should wait on that until after they'd dealt with the King.

❖

The watcher, peering out from behind the fountain, saw the short woman pause beside the bench where the noblewoman he'd been watching usually sat and knitted. The woman stopped and bent down. She seemed to be retying her shoelace. Then, out of the corner of his eye, the watcher caught movement back in the direction of the earl's front gate. The noblewoman he was concerned with had begun crossing the square, carefully avoiding the small puddles that had formed amongst the cobblestones. As she reached the bench and sat down in her usual position, her bag of knitting in her lap, she looked inquisitively at the short woman who still remained by the end of the bench.

It was clear to the watcher that a few words had been exchanged by the pair of women, but he was too far distant to make them out. Then the short woman gave the noblewoman a tiny curtsy and scuttled toward the central stairsteps, probably going to her job up at the castle.

The watcher was tired. He'd been at his post since midnight. This constant surveillance was boring and exhausting, and after two weeks it had produced nothing. There was no trace of the man they sought. Surely he wasn't at Earl Thomas's home. This was a wild goose chase, pure and simple. But he'd keep on doing his job. No need to provoke his betters.

Skipping down the steps from the castle came the young noblewoman he'd seen the day before. He couldn't help admiring her quick and graceful movements, her slim and attractive body. At least keeping his eyes on these two lovely women offered some compensation.

Nimuë's eye caught sight of a small bit of folded parchment that lay behind the back leg of the bench on which Juliana sat. She wondered what it was and why it was there. But for the moment she ignored it. She knew they were being watched.

After an exchange of cheerful greetings, the two women got quickly down to business with their knitting, not bothering with small talk. Nimuë had brought some beautiful yarn, and she was quick at learning the intricate pattern Juliana demonstrated for her.

"To begin with," Nimuë said, "I'm just going to try to make a simple tippet or perhaps a shawl. When I really get the knack of it, I'll try for something more challenging."

"You've pretty much got it already, seems to me," Juliana said. "Gracious, that was quick."

"Yes, I've always had nimble fingers. M'lady," she said lowering her voice, "are you familiar with the knight Sir Pelleas?"

Juliana hesitated a moment before replying. Then she said cautiously, "I know *of* him, though I've never met him." She'd suspected there was something odd about this young woman's sudden appearance yesterday, and that there might be more to it than just her wanting to have a knitting lesson.

"He's concerned about the King," Nimuë continued. "He loves and admires the King, and, to put it bluntly, he loathes the Prince Regent. I hope you can keep that a secret." Juliana nodded. "We believe the King is coming back. And if we are right, Sir Pelleas and a few others intend to aid him in his return. We intend to try to thwart the malicious designs of the Prince. M'lady, Sir Pelleas especially wants to find Earl Thomas's nephew, the man who is the young Earl of Sanham. His name is Lute. We hope to have his assistance. Apparently, Sir Pelleas isn't the *only* one who wishes to find him," she said, nodding in the direction of the watcher who was skulking behind the fountain.

"No, he isn't."

"M'lady, if you know any way to contact him, could you let him know that he has an ally in Sir Pelleas? Working together, perhaps they can protect the King upon his return."

Juliana decided that at this point she had better be noncommittal. She just nodded and remained silent.

Nimuë placed her knitting down and stood up to stretch. She walked a circuit around the bench, then stopped by the far end of the bench and quickly scooped up the small fragment of folded parchment the other woman had dropped there earlier. She handed it to Juliana. "This, I think, is intended for you. I suggest you hide it quickly."

Giving it hardly a glance, Juliana slipped it into her knitting bag. "Now let me show you just one more stitch," she said loudly.

"Oh, yes, please do," Nimuë replied.

Chapter 20

Lute, wearing an old cloak of Gwilym's, stood just behind the entrance gate in the small front garden of Earl Thomas's home. He listened to the night sounds while he waited for his eyes to adjust to the darkness. The note Mary had left for Juliana indicated that he should be in the Minster's nave that night just as the service of matins was beginning. That was what he hoped to do, though he knew it might not be so simple getting there. It wasn't likely that his feeble disguise—consisting of one of Gwilym's old cloaks and a walking stick—would fool anyone.

After a five-minute wait, Lute unlatched the gate and stepped through. He slipped quickly into a well-shadowed spot along the front wall where again he stood and listened. He heard nothing other than the sound of a night bird calling from a tree over on the far side of the square. He saw no one. The square seemed deserted.

Using the walking stick and doing his best to imitate Gwilym's aged stoop, he began moving in the direction of the central stairsteps. He was nearly there when a loud voice cried out, "Stop! Sir, you must *stop!*"

Lute did.

The watcher, who had seen the stooped figure of Gwilym many times before, had been puzzled by the sight of this person crossing the square at this hour of the night. What would he be doing out at such a time? And stooped over as he was, the man still looked a good bit taller than normal. What was that that hung by his left side beneath his cloak? Was that a sword? The old man the watcher had seen before had never carried a sword.

"Throw back your hood and let me see your face," the watcher demanded as he approached. The watcher had now unsheathed his sword. He'd better take this fellow into custody.

At the same time, Lute tossed back his hood and he, too, drew his sword.

"Ah, ha!" the watcher declared, "you're a game one, eh? Well, let's see how game you are." He proffered a blow at Lute's sword hand. But before it landed, the man felt a hard blow on his own wrist. His sword clattered down onto the cobblestones. In a flash, he'd been unarmed. He was stunned and amazed. Now he felt a sword tip at his throat.

"Leave your weapon where it lies," Lute said sternly. "Don't try to follow me. You do, and I'll do more than just unarm you. Return to your post and continue your surveillance, and no one will be the wiser. You saw nothing unusual tonight. Do you understand?"

"I do," the man said. "I ain't seen nothin' out of the ordinary the whole blessed night through." With his left hand he rubbed at the broken skin and the red welt that was swelling up on his right wrist. His sword lay on the cobblestones. He didn't dare reach for it.

Lute spun around. No longer walking with a stoop, he hurried toward the central stairsteps. He glanced back once to be sure he wasn't being followed.

The bells had just finished sounding for matins when Lute slipped through the north porch entrance and into the minster's dark nave. It was dimly illuminated by the light of just a few candles.

"Lute!" came a whispered voice, which Lute recognized as Tom's. Tom beckoned him toward a well-shadowed corner. In the choir beyond the chancel arch, the monks had begun singing the appropriate psalms for the matins service.

"Were you seen?" came another voice, as Lute arrived at the appointed spot.

"Yes," Lute replied.

"Then we must get you away at once."

"Lute," Tom said, "this is Sir Pelleas."

"Hello, sir," Lute said. "I guessed as much."

"Do you know the small postern gate at the top left-hand side of the curtain wall?" Sir Pelleas asked.

"I do. There was a time when I rode through that gate regularly."

"The guards there are with us. At my say-so, they will let you through. Here, wear this." He tossed a very fine cloak to Lute to replace Gwilym's humble garb.

"Lute, is Raguel with our friend the farmer?" Tom

asked. "Merlyn wants *me* to ride him. He doesn't want you to ride him ever again." Lute couldn't help smiling, though it was too dark for the others to see.

"I'm sure he doesn't."

"Lute, I have a very good mount for you," Sir Pelleas said. "Tom, we will all assemble there at the farm before prime tomorrow morning."

"I guess that means we know where we are going," Lute said.

"Yes, thanks to Nimuë we do."

"A little bird told her?" Tom said.

"Yes," Sir Pelleas replied, "something along those lines."

"How many of us are there?" Lute asked.

"About fifty."

"How many knights do you think the King still has?"

"We think about twenty-five."

"And what is the size of Mordred's cavalry?"

"We think about 250, once they've all been brought together from their disparate locations."

"I don't much like them numbers," Tom said, with a shake of his head.

"The king also has about 100 foot-soldiers."

"Who will be easy fodder for Mordred's horse-soldiers," Tom said.

"Yes, that's probably so. Well, Lute, we'd best be going."

Lute donned the cloak. As he exited the minster, he dropped Gwilym's old wrap down beside the poor box.

❖

"The boy," Queen Margause said, "you must see to him."

"He's a worthless little louse," Mordred replied. "I can't believe he's Lute's flesh and blood. Colgrevaunce must have brought the wrong boy."

"In any case, you must see to him. If the people grow too fond of him, it could spell trouble. Your plan to use the boy to draw Lute obviously hasn't worked. The boy has no value to us, but he could be a danger. Make him disappear, quickly and quietly. He probably hasn't wormed his way too deeply into people's hearts just yet. After a few days I'm sure they will have forgotten him."

Magdalene had just come into the room to take away the tray containing the woman's breakfast dishes. She'd caught the last bit of this conversation—"make him disappear, quickly and quietly." She knew the woman couldn't be talking about Lute, so she must mean the little boy. A chill ran through her heart.

"Anything more, m'lady?" Magdalene asked her. Mar-gause, not even deigning to make a spoken reply, gave a dismissive wave of her hand. As Mags exited the chamber, she heard the woman exclaim once more, "Do it! Do it tonight!"

Magdalene knew she had to try to help the boy. But how? Then she had a thought.

❖

Before daybreak, Lute reached the farm outside the city where he'd left Raguel. Sir Pelleas had been right about the guards at the upper postern gate. They'd allowed him to pass through at Sir Pelleas's say-so, and one of the older ones even remembered Lute from nearly a decade ago.

"Good to see you again, sir," he'd said. "It's been a good long while."

"It has," Lute replied.

"I'll never forget that day we saw you come riding in in the company of the King. He seemed so fond of you, sir."

"It was quite a thrill for me, too. It was the first time I'd ever met him."

"Well, sir, be safe," the guard said, as Lute departed.

"Thank you. I hope I'll see you again. Maybe next time in less than ten years."

"That would be grand, sir. God go with you."

At the farm, Lute left his new horse in one stall and then secreted himself in the stall where the farmer had placed Raguel—a stall as far removed from his other horses as any he had. Lute spoke softly to the great stallion and rubbed his neck. "Merlyn says I'm not to ride you anymore. But he didn't say we couldn't share a stall." The horse gave a little snort. Then Lute smoothed a spot for himself in the straw. He was in need of a nap. It had been an eventful night, and there was every likelihood the next few days would be even more eventful. Today, he would stay completely out of sight and get rested up. Lute knew that before daybreak tomorrow, the knights who still supported the King would be gathering. Then they would set off together for wherever it was Nimuë believed the King would make his landing. Lute wondered if she would travel with them. He was yet to meet this young woman.

❖

As usual, Yonec accompanied Simon to the minster for his afternoon studies. While the boy was in the cloisters studying with the other lads, Yonec planned to run some errands down on the lowest level of the city. As he descended the long set of steps, he didn't realize he was being followed.

The central market square was crowded on this weekday afternoon, and a great many folks were clustered about the first market stall he needed to visit. As he waited patiently, he felt a tug at his elbow. He turned and looked into a slightly familiar face. It was the face of a woman he'd seen working up at the castle.

"Young sir," she said quietly, "I have a message for you. From the Prince Regent. It's about the boy. Come over by the fountain and I will deliver it."

Yonec was flummoxed by her words, but he followed as she stepped quickly toward the center of the square. She stopped and leaned against the edge of the waist-high wall that surrounded the fountain. Yonec was soon there beside her. He looked at her expectantly.

The woman put her hand into her bag and partially extracted a small dagger—just far enough that the young squire could see what she held. "The Prince," she said, "has an assignment for you." The youth stared at the woman. She stared back. "He wants you to dispose of the boy."

Yonec was staggered by her statement. His face

couldn't conceal his astonishment. Finally he said, "He wants me to do *what?*"

"He needs you to dispose of the boy. He'd like you to make it look like an accident. Could you do that?"

"Kill the boy? No, miss, I *couldn't* do that. Why in the world would I? That would be a horrible thing to do."

She stared at him for a moment. "You would refuse a direct order of the Prince Regent?"

Yonec hesitated. "Umm . . . not usually, miss . . . but this one . . . , I'm afraid I would."

The woman looked into his face without speaking, judging the sincerity of his words. "I am glad to hear you say that, Yonec," she said at last. "It *is* what the Prince wants. But it isn't what I want. And it certainly isn't what Sir Pelleas wants."

"Sir Pelleas?"

"He wants you to take the boy and put him somewhere safe. He wants you to keep him out of harm's way until the Prince has departed."

"The Prince and his men are going off to where the King and his knights are landing?"

"Yes, and very soon." Yonec nodded. This information was not a surprise to him. He'd known it was coming. "If you can keep the lad safely hidden for the next couple of days," she said, "then we'll see where things stand."

Yonec wasn't certain that he could trust this woman. Who was she? She wasn't a high-born woman. How could she know what the Prince Regent intended?

Nonetheless, he thought there was a good chance she

knew whereof she spoke. She seemed to truly care about the lad. She seemed sincere. He would go and collect the boy as usual after his lessons and then return to the citadel. And he would keep his eyes peeled.

Yonec did know of a secret place where he could hide the boy. If he caught even the tiniest whiff of danger, he decided, he would take the boy there. Yonec had never liked or trusted the Prince Regent. If Sir Pelleas, whom he greatly admired, really wanted the boy protected, he would do everything in his power to do that.

❖

"It's the Sabrina Sea, my lord. Close to the village of Burnham."

"Burnham Sands? In Somerset?"

"Yes, my lord, that's the place."

"Have messages been sent to all the commanders?"

"They have, my lord."

"Excellent. How soon can our knights here in the city be ready to set off?"

"They are ready now, sire."

"Excellent. I just need to tidy up a couple of little matters, and then I'll be ready as well. If we can make a start by late afternoon, we could ride until dark. What will it take us, two and a half days?"

"If there are no unexpected delays."

"Then let's not have any."

Mordred was excited. Things were coming to a head. His cavalry, he felt sure, would be far superior to the tattered remnants of the King's forces, and the journey to Burnham shouldn't be too exhausting. If all went well, they should have everything concluded within a week or so. By then it would be December, and his Christmas coronation could occur just as he and his mother had hoped.

One of the small matters he still needed to sort out was the boy. That was rather a pain in the backside, but it had to be dealt with. Perhaps he could entrust that responsibility to Osmond, his chamberlain. Mordred believed the vile fellow would enjoy ridding them of the fat little slug. Mordred's own animosity toward Simon had grown ever greater as the boy failed to take any interest at all in chivalry, knighthood, or kingship. The little slug preferred knowing about birds and flowers and starry constellations. And *books*. The little wretch was truly an embarrassment, an ugly blemish that needed removing. Yes, Osmond was just the man for the job, the cold-blooded bastard. Mordred couldn't help smiling as he thought about Osmond attending to the boy.

After Agravaine, Colgrevaunce, and the others had departed from Mordred's private chamber, Osmond secured the door behind them.

"Osmond," Mordred said, "there's a special duty I'd like you to perform for me, this evening if possible. It's something, I think, that you might enjoy."

"Does it involve the boy, sire?" he asked, his almost lipless mouth forming a malicious grin.

"How did you know?"

"Sire, I saw this coming days ago."

"You're good with taking care of the matter?"

"Sire, it would my pleasure."

❖

Simon wasn't the only one who'd been learning Latin during the last few weeks. Ever since he'd become one of Rob's "sons," Matthew, along with Rob's son John, had been amongst a small cluster of pupils studying each day with Father Andreas, the local curate. At first Matt hadn't been too keen on these daily sessions, but the intricacies of the language soon fascinated him and he was on his way to becoming a fledgling scholar. He and John were soon competing for the honor of being best in class.

Part of the appeal to Matthew of his daily studies stemmed from the person of the youthful curate. He wasn't some dry-as-dust old scholar, he was a strapping and athletic young clergyman who regularly joined the students in their post-lesson football sessions on the village green. He firmly subscribed to the *mens sana in corpore sana* philosophy. He'd impressed the boy by being able to dribble the ball skillfully with either foot, as well as by the fact that he wasn't shy about occasionally letting slip a good, mouth-filling oath.

During a session one day, Andreas asked his pupils if they had any questions about the perfect case of verbs. Matt slowly raised a hand. The young curate nodded encouragement and Matt said, "The verb *fecit*, sir, I'm not sure what it means."

"Could you use it in a sentence?"

"Umm, I read a phrase once that said, '*M. fecit.*' I didn't understand what that meant."

"*Fecit* is the past tense of the third-person singular form of the verb *facio*. It means 'to do' or 'to make.' You often find it written at the end of works of literature. It's how an author may take credit for his work. He's saying, 'Andreas made this'. Sometimes it refers to the scribe rather than to the author. In the case of your example, it probably means that someone whose name begins with the letter M 'did this.' Does that make sense, Matthew? I'm wondering where you encountered this phrase?"

The boy preferred not to say where he'd seen the phrase—it was a phrase he'd seen inscribed in the flesh of his father's chest—so he just shrugged and mumbled, "Umm, I can't quite remember." The curate looked at him doubtfully. But not wanting to embarrass the boy, he let the matter drop. Matthew wasn't about to say that he'd seen those words carved into his father's body. Apparently, based on the curate's explanation, someone whose name began with M had done that to his father's body with a razor-sharp blade. Lute never talked about the scars on his chest with his son. Knowing the literal meaning of the phrase only made Matthew even more curious about those scars than he'd been before.

END GAME

Chapter 21

Many small tents lay scattered on the seaward side of a line of high dunes. In their midst on the sandy beach loomed two larger pavilions. Driftwood fires sent slender smoke plumes skyward. Men clustered about the largest of the fires speaking in low, subdued tones. Their faces were drawn and anxious.

"The other ships," one of them said, "any notion as to their fates?" The speaker was a tall man in early middle age. Fines lines fanned out from around his eyes and his light-brown hair bore traces of gray. The man was Arthur, the King of Britain.

"I saw one founder," a second man said, "two others were still afloat. They could yet arrive safely." This speaker was Sir Ewen, a slender young man who was one of the King's few surviving nephews and one of Arthur's most trusted supporters.

"Pray that they do," Arthur replied, "for their sakes, and for ours—if there's any truth to those rumors we'd been hearing."

"Sire, I think I see one of them now," said a third man. His name was Sir Phineus. A much older man with a grizzled beard, he'd been scanning the horizon, his hand shielding his eyes.

All heads turned and gazed at the rough and rumpled-looking surface of the sea. A large carrack hove into view, moving slowly around the spit of land that extended out into the sea to their left. It wallowed toward the shore, its masts and riggings hanging in tatters. But, gloriously, it was still afloat.

"It's the *Mathias*," said Sir Ewen. "Foot soldiers and horses. Lord knows we may well need them."

"After they've landed, get them settled," the King said. "Later, we'll take stock of things. Keep an eye out for that last ship. If Providence smiles on us, it will arrive safely also."

"Been awhile since Providence smiled on us," muttered another man beneath his breath.

"Means we're overdue for some good fortune," replied the man beside him, also speaking in a low voice. The two stood slightly apart from the King and the three men huddled closest around him.

"Always the optimist, eh Saggie?"

The man who was speaking was Sir Gomber. The man he'd called Saggie was Sir Sagramour, a celebrated knight from Constantinople.

"What's the latest on Sir Gawaine?" Sir Sagramour asked.

"He was still holding on, last I heard. Getting tossed and tumbled in that bloody sea storm surely didn't do his head wounds any good, that's for sure."

"For the King's sake, I hope he survives. There's no

one in the world the King loves more."

"Don't ever underestimate Sir Gawaine. He may not be the smartest or the most skillful amongst us, but no one's made of sterner stuff."

"I can't disagree with that," replied Sir Sagramour.

❖

In Lute's absence, Jillian had turned the everyday running of things over to Brogan. He handled all the routine matters at the manor ably on his own, though he always consulted her on matters of consequence.

The one sour note in all that had been happening there was the schism between Willikyn and Eldred. Brogan thought the ill will between the two friends would subside in a week or so, but it hadn't. Even Jillian noticed it.

After the day's chores were finished, Brogan summoned the two of them out behind the manor's large barn to the small stone hut where the workers stored their tools. A turf fire burned in the crude fireplace dispelling the late afternoon's chill.

"Listen here, you two," Brogan said gruffly, "I've had enough of this. Time for you two to knock it the hell off. Your little feud is upsetting things. We can't have that, not no more, we can't."

"This here bugger," Willikyn said, jerking a thumb toward Eldred, "I hates workin' with 'im."

"Why's that, Willikyn?"

Willikyn hesitated, then said, "You tell 'im, Eldred. Not for me to say."

"Eldred?" Brogan said, turning to the other man for

an explanation.

Eldred fidgeted, swaying back and forth slightly, his hands held clasped in front of him. Finally he said, "It's my fault, Brog, I'm the one who messed up."

"Tell me what happened."

"It were me, Brog. I were the one who let them fellers know that little Matt was holed up at old Wat's farm. It were me what spilled the beans. But Brog, them fellas was really a-hurtin' me—"

"Pah!" spat out Willikyn.

"They *was*, I swear it. And more was a-comin'. But I still shoulda took it. I were a coward, that's what I were."

"Damn right ya were," said Willikyn. "Ya weren't man enough ta endure it."

"Well, they didn't get him," said Brogan. "That's the important thing. Ya shouldn't've blabbed, Eldred, ya owed the Earl more loyalty than that. But, ya didn't do no worse than many men woulda done."

"If there's a next time, Brog, I'll do better."

"Ha," scoffed Willikyn. "I'll believe that when I sees it."

"I promise ya, on me mum's grave."

"And you, my man," Brogan said sternly addressing Willikyn, "you need to give your friend here another chance. He knows he messed up. Listen to me—we need the two of yous working together for the sake of the manor, for the sake of Lute and Lady Jillian, and all of us. Can you do that? Will you do that?"

Slowly, Willikyn nodded his agreement. So did Eldred.

"A man who can't forgive his friend ain't much of a man," Brogan said, looking pointedly at Willikyn.

Willikyn nodded sheepishly.

Tom, on Raguel, and Nimuë, on a sleek bay palfrey, rode well apart from the others in the long cavalcade. A group of six knights comprised the vanguard, followed by the main body of knights, about sixty in all, riding two by two. Then came Tom and Nimuë, the only two riders who didn't fit in neatly with the others. Behind them rode six knights comprising the rearguard. Lute and Sir Pelleas rode at the head of the main group.

The riders in the vanguard moved along at a good clip. The cavalcade had set out before sunrise on this early December morn. By their mid-day break, they'd already traveled quite a few miles. The route they traveled ran parallel to the coast, though in order to cross the powerful and swift-flowing Sabrina River they would soon reach, they would have to go inland a good ways in order to find a suitable fording spot. The lead riders knew where that would be. They planned to halt for the night either just before crossing the river, or, if the tide were right, just afterward. It all depended on the timing of the tidal flow.

As they rode, Tom tried to engage Nimuë in conversation. He knew little about her except that she'd had some sort of friendship with Merlyn—he wasn't quite sure what—and he tried delicately to probe that topic. Merlyn meant a great deal to him—indeed, he owed the man his life—and Tom cared greatly about the old man's well-being. He knew well Merlyn's various susceptibilities, and he knew that this very smart, very attractive young woman possessed qualities that posed a great danger for the old fellow. He also knew that Merlyn had always believed he was fated to fall prey to someone rather like her. Was she the one? And was that likely to happen soon? Or, had it *already* happened? Tom hadn't had any contact with Merlyn since before their rescue of little Matthew, several weeks back.

Nimuë was quite affable, Tom thought, but all the same, she was rather guarded in her responses to his questions. She gave little away. She already seemed to know a good bit about Tom's relationship to the old man, though she didn't reveal much about her own. She deflected the conversation away from Merlyn, by asking Tom questions about the great black horse, Raguel. She wanted to know why Tom was one of the few who could ride the creature, and why the horse seemed to make all the other horses nervous whenever they came near him.

Trying to be facetious, Tom joked that Raguel was "nothin' more than the Devil's own steed," something the other horses could sense. "People, too," he said, "often feel evil emanatin' from the critter, though they don't know what it is 'bout 'im makes 'em so jittery."

"I've had similar feelings," she said, "though the creature doesn't frighten me the way he does others. Is that why Merlyn doesn't want Lute to ride the horse, because of its associations with the Devil?"

"Ye ma'am, that's pretty much it."

"But what about you, Tom? Are you impervious to evil?"

"*Me*? Oh, m'lady, when it comes to evil, I ain't nuthin' but a lost cause, so there ain't no harm in my ridin' on Rags. I've had close associations with the Devil my whole worthless life through. There was a time when I probably coulda taught Old Nick a trick or two myself. Not no more, though, now Merlyn's gone and got me all straightened around." Tom laughed heartily. Raguel chimed in with a loud snort.

❖

Even though he missed his grandfather's simple, countrified cooking, Simon's appetite hadn't diminished, Osmond noted. What a detestable little slug the boy was, the man thought. Well, he would put an end to that tonight. It would be a relief to have him removed permanently from the royal apartments.

"It's going to be a clear, moonless night tonight, Simon," Osmond said to the boy after he returned from removing the boy's supper dishes. "How would you like to do some stargazing?"

"Oh, that would be wonderful."

"I think the Prince would be fine with our going up atop the highest tower tonight. We could be sure of having it all to ourselves."

"The highest one? Oh my, I've never been up that one. Right there below King Uther's great banner! Oh, thank you, sir. That would be grand."

They waited a couple hours until the sky above the

city was as dark as it would get. Osmond was right—the night would be moonless until much later. They carried small torches to light their way.

Osmond led them through several passageways until they reached the closed doorway to the entrance to the tower's staircase. A guard nodded at Osmond and stepped aside as the odd pair entered. The many steps made an arduous climb for the chubby little boy, and he was out of breath by the time they reached the top. A chest-high wall with a few widely spaced crenellations encircled the small open area at the top of the tower. Simon placed his elbows on it and panted noisily. He looked up at the great banner, which loomed above them in the darkness.

They stood in silence for a while, both of them taking in the great swath of stars that blazed across the night sky. As he caught his breath, Simon stared down at the rooftops of the city. He'd never seen the city from this height before or this late at night. Although a scattering of small lights twinkled beneath him—coming from the windows of houses, shops, and churches—the city was largely bathed in darkness. The sight evoked a sense of awe in the boy.

"You are the expert and I am just a novice," Osmond said, "so I want you to teach me about the constellations. Have you caught your breath? You aren't too cold, are you?" he asked, solicitously. "I've brought an extra shawl if you need it."

"Thank you, sir, but the climb has warmed me quite a lot."

Above them, the heavens seemed awash in dazzling stars. To the boy it was a familiar sight. He'd often sat on a blanket beside his grandfather in the grassy field back of the farm and studied this same sky. Suddenly an even brighter light shot across his vision from left to right. It disappeared in less than a second. Simon smiled. Osmond didn't say anything, so he probably hadn't seen it. Well, if he hadn't, then it was his loss.

"The constellations?" Osmond said at last. "Would you point some of them out?"

"Ursa Minor," Simon said, pointing at the Little Dipper. Do you see the star at the bottom of the line of 'em? That's Stella Maris. She's the Pole Star. She doesn't move. The others swing about her in a circle."

"Ah, I see the one you mean."

"Do you see the group of stars a bit lower and to the left that kind of form a double V? That's Cassiopeia," Simon said pointing overhead in a slightly northern direction. "Do you see her?"

"Yes, I do see her. Simon, your knowledge is most impressive."

Simon then pointed out the constellations of Perseus and Andromeda. "Oh, my, they are lovely," Osmond said, feigning an interest in the subject, though his thoughts had already turned to the plan he'd hatched involving the boy's demise, a plan he intended to carry out here, tonight.

"Come over and stand next to me, Simon," the man said. "It's my turn to show you something quite wonderful." He led the boy to one of the lower openings in parapet's crenellations. Here the protective wall was only waist-high rather than chest-high. Here one could lean out and have a very fine view of the castle gardens far below. Tonight the gardens were mostly in darkness, though far below them a few well-spaced flambeaux illumined the surrounding path.

"It's a lovely sight, sir," the boy said, leaning out and starring downward. Surprisingly, he seemed to have no fear of heights. Suddenly, Simon felt two strong hands gripping his ankles. He was being lifted up. His body was being thrust out over the parapet. Then the hands released him.

Yonec, shielded behind a support pillar, had watched as Osmond and Simon left the Prince's apartments and set off for the entrance to the high tower. He'd trailed behind them cautiously, and he'd been close by when the guard allowed them to pass through the door to tower's staircase. He himself had never been permitted to climb that tower. He knew he wouldn't be able to get past the guard so he didn't try. He very much feared that Osmond had evil intentions, but he knew there was nothing he could do about it. He felt impotent. He would wait quietly and hope for the best. Maybe, in half an hour or so, the pair would come back through the door. They surely wouldn't stay up there in the chilly night air for much longer than that. As that thought was in his mind, he heard the scream.

The guard had heard it, too. He hesitated only a moment before flinging the door wide and dashing through. Yonec didn't hesitate. He dashed through the door as well. He could hear the guard's footsteps ascending the stone steps above him as he charged upward.

When Yonec reached the top, he saw the guard standing over a body propped against the wall of the parapet. It was Osmond.

The boy? Where was the boy?

Chapter 22

The guard was looking down at Osmond, leaning against the parapet wall. Blood was spreading across the stones beneath Osmond's feet. Osmond moaned. The boy, Yonec wondered, where was he?

"This is going to hurt like the devil," the guard said. Osmond continued to moan. The guard removed a sash from around his waist. "Now!" he cried. Osmond screamed in agony. Using his sash, the guard tried to stem the sudden gush of blood from Osmond's thigh.

Yonec stared at the dagger the guard held in his hand. It was the same dagger the woman had given him earlier to "dispose of the boy"; the same one he'd passed on to the boy to provide him a small measure of protection. It was the one the boy, having no sheath, had shoved beneath his belt, mimicking the way he'd seen country farmhands sometimes carry their knives. Had the boy used it on Osmond? He must have. But where *was* the boy, and who had screamed? The boy? Or Osmond when Simon plunged the knife into his thigh?

Finally, Yonec saw the boy huddled in the darkness.

He was all scrunched up on the floor stones directly beneath the pole on which hung Uther Pendragon's great banner. He was shivering and shaking.

Yonec helped Simon to his feet and began pulling him toward the opening to the tower steps. They must get away while the guard was still attending to Osmond. Despite Simon being in a state of shock, Yonec hurried him down the steep steps. He decided he wouldn't try to hide him in the place he'd thought of earlier. He would get him all the way out of the citadel tonight. The woman he'd talked to during the day said she might be able to help them. Yonec knew where to find her.

An hour later, Simon was sitting in the warm kitchen at the back of the chandler's shop. A woman who said her name was Mary had placed a steaming bowl of leek-and-lintel soup on the table in front of him, along with several hunks of fresh warm bread.

Simon was still quite shaken by the events up on the high tower. He was frightened and confused. He didn't know this woman. She said she was a friend of Tom's, whom he remembered from events at his grandfather's farm. The smell of her soup made him think of his grandfather's cooking. As shaken as he was, he found that he was able to eat a few bites. And as he relaxed and returned to a semblance of his regular self, Simon discovered he much preferred Mary's simple fare to the more refined delicacies Osmond had provided up at the castle.

❖

The solitary rider threaded his way through the sand dunes, guided by the plumes of smoke he could see rising from the campfires on the beach. He'd been riding hard for two days. He felt sure he was at least half a day ahead of Mordred's troops. It was vital that he get here well before them.

He pulled up as the guards posted at the edge of the dunes motioned for him to stop. "Sir Craddock?" one of them suddenly said. "Is that you?"

"It's me, Sir Dodinas. And I'm very relieved to see you well."

"I'm not sure how well you see me. But you've obviously been pushing your noble steed quite hard. You've brought a message for the King?"

"I have. Can you direct me to him?"

Sir Dodinas pointed toward the largest of the pavilions. "I hope your news is good."

"No, it isn't, but it's urgent. So having a proper visit with you, my friend, will have to wait."

Sir Dodinas nodded and motioned for Sir Craddock to ride on.

The cluster of knights gathered outside the King's pavilion watched as the rider approached. "Sir Craddock!" one of them shouted.

"Sir Lucan," he replied. "Happy to see you. Sir, I need to see the King. It's urgent."

And then there he was. Having heard the voices, the King stepped forward through the pavilion's opening to greet this knight for whom he'd always had a high regard.

"Sire," Sir Craddock said. He climbed down from his mound and kneeled before the King.

"Arise, sir knight. Come. Shall we have a bite as we talk? You must be hungry. You bring news?"

"Alas, sire, I do, and there's little time to spare."

As they ate, Sir Craddock brought the King up to date on what had been happening in Britain. In particular, he warned him of the imminent arrival of Mordred and his cavalry.

"Mordred has convinced the people that you are dead, sire. He's planning his own coronation for Christmas. The people, for the most part, have accepted him. Although they regret the news of your demise, some folks feel that you deserted them, putting your personal interests ahead of theirs."

"There's some truth to that," the King remarked glumly.

"Few people know that you've returned. Mordred wants to make sure it stays that way. Indeed, sire, he wants to make sure you don't remain alive."

"It seems the rumors we'd been hearing are true," the King said. His face bore a grimace. "I guess I should have known. Well, how soon will they be here?"

"Probably by nightfall. It's likely they won't attack until tomorrow."

"Do you think Mordred might be amenable to negotiation?"

"Perhaps. But sire, he has proved himself to be most untrustworthy. You must prepare yourself for all eventualities."

"Are we entirely on our own?"

"Not entirely, but nearly. Sir Pelleas has assembled a small force of those still loyal to you. They're on their way now. They probably aren't too far behind Mordred's cavalry."

The King smiled at the mention of Sir Pelleas. "A fine young fellow," he said.

"And there's another youngish fellow with him—someone I don't know much about. He's the Earl of Sanham, goes by the name of Lute."

"*Lute?* So, Lute is coming, too? Sir Craddock, that's the best news I've heard since returning to Britain's shores. So Lute is coming, too. That touches my heart."

Sir Craddock couldn't help wondering about the King's surprising, inexplicable comments. Who, he wondered, was this Lute fellow?

"Sire, we should take the high ground," said Sir Ewen.

"Atop the Knoll?"

"As quickly as possible, sire."

"I concur," said Sir Sagramour. "Those ancient earthworks will give us some protection. And forcing them to charge uphill will blunt the impact of their cavalry."

"Good," said the King. "Then let's make it so."

The movement of their encampment was soon underway, and by late afternoon they had shifted everyone—knights, horses, footsoldiers—to behind the earthen ramparts of the ancient enclosure high atop the small mountain known as Brent Knoll.

"Lute," Tom said, studying a set of horse tracks, "They're about half a day ahead of us."

"The King should know about them by now," Sir Pelleas said. "Craddock will have informed him. If so, he'll be ready for them. Maybe he'll try to buy time by negotiating with Mordred, in which case we might get there before any real fighting breaks out."

"Do you think Mordred knows about us?" Lute asked.

"It's likely. But I doubt if he's much worried about us. Probably assumes our force is essentially negligible."

"Is it?" Tom asked.

"Pretty much," Sir Pelleas said.

"No," Nimuë said, "it isn't."

"Well, I'm glad someone thinks that," Tom said. "If Mordred's cavalry is as strong a unit as it's described, it sounds like it would take a minor miracle for us to have much effect on things."

"The wonderful thing about miracles," Nimuë said, "is that they sometimes occur."

Tom grinned. "Is that so? Then let's hope this is one of those times."

CHAPTER 23

During his first few weeks with Rob's family, Matthew hadn't seen much of his grandmother. Most often he saw her at the village church services on Sunday morning, and sometimes when he did, he joined her on her regular pew. The woman intrigued the boy, and he longed to have greater contact with her. An idea began to take shape in his head.

"Sir," Matt said to Rob one evening, "when I was in Sanham, I had just begun to learn the art of woodworking. I would really like to keep doing that. Do you think you could teach me?"

"I'm no dab hand," Rob replied, "but I do have a little experience with it. At the least, I could let you have a few tools you could practice with. Is there something you've a mind to work on?"

"Yes, sir, there is. I was thinking of making a Christmas present for my mother—something not so difficult that I couldn't do most of the work myself. I was thinking that I might try and make her a small serving tray."

"That's an excellent idea, Matt. Tell you what. Out

in the shed I have quite a few scraps of different kinds of wood. You go look 'em over. See if you think one of 'em might suit your purposes. You can help yourself to anything you find there."

"Thank you, sir."

An hour later Matthew was hard at work. Using a chisel and small mallet, he began shaping an irregular scrap of cherry wood into a rectangle about two feet long and a foot wide. When the boy had roughed it out, Rob showed him how to gouge out the middle section leaving a raised border about two inches wide around the edges. Then Matt set about planing the center of the rectangle, getting it as flat and level as he could make it. Using the rough stems of horsetail weeds as an abrasive, he smoothed down all the surfaces further. For a week, he sanded and smoothed the piece of wood for a few hours each evening.

Johnny, seeing what Matt was doing, grew envious. Before long, he too was hard at work on a project of his own. The competitiveness of the two boys spurred them on, which amused Rob. It's just like Lute 'n' me in the old days, he thought with a smile.

Matt knew that Neely intended to return to Sanham a few days before Christmas to visit a young lady friend of his. And Matt knew he could get Neely to carry the present to his mother, if only he could get it finished. It hadn't taken him long to complete the basic tray, but the most important parts of the project still lay ahead. For them, the boy wanted his grandmother's assistance. Having a good reason for spending more time with her had been a central part of his plan all along.

After the church service the following Sunday, his grandmother invited Matt to have a meal with her. He accepted eagerly. He was nervous about being on his own with her for the whole afternoon, but she quickly set him at ease by asking him to perform a few small chores for her—collecting eggs from the nests in her small hen house; moving the goat's tether to a fresh grassy area beyond the horse enclosure. Gathering eggs was one of his regular chores back home in Sanham, though there they had no goats.

As they were just finishing their meal of pot roast, bread, and cheese, Matt said, "Grandmother, I've been making a present for my mother. It's a serving tray." Lyonore smiled and nodded approvingly. "But there's still one thing I need to do. I want to put some simple designs all around the raised edge of the tray."

"Do you have an idea of the designs you'd like to make?"

"Yes, ma'am, I do." Matthew stepped over to the sideboard and picked up the wooden bowl he knew Watt had made for her many years earlier. "Grandmother, I would like to try and make something similar to these. Do you think that's possible?"

"I do, Matt. But it will require patience and care to do it well."

"I'd like to try and see if I could carve the signs of the zodiac into the raised border." He ran his fingers over the incised designs. "I'd like to make figures similar to Watt's, 'cept I want the faces to resemble people I know—Neely and Brogan, Willykin and Wat."

"Anyone else?"

"Maybe my friend Simon. Oh, of course my sister Editha. And my mother and father, for sure."

"That sounds wonderful, but it won't be easy. I could help you with the likenesses, if you wish."

"Grandmother, I was hoping you would."

"I have a special little tool, it's a kind of knife that I think would work well for carving the faces."

"Grandmother, there's one more person I would really like to include."

"And who is that?"

"My grandfather. But Grandmother, I've never actually seen him. Could you describe him to me and help me with his face? I was thinking for him I would use the sign of Leo." Lyonore blanched. Matthew's question had caught her completely off guard.

"Umm, do you mean your mother's father?" she said at last, being pretty certain that *wasn't* who he meant. "He and your grandmother lived just on the other side of the village, no more than two miles from here. I saw them often. So yes, I could describe him."

"I do remember him a little bit. But Grandmother, he's not the one I was asking about. I was asking about my other grandfather, my father's father. My father rarely speaks of him, though I know he much admires him. Maybe you could tell me about him. What he looks like, but also tell me more about him as a man."

"Matthew . . . ," she said, followed by a lengthy pause, "if you really want to know what he looks like—or what he once looked like—I could show you a small painting I made a long time ago. Back then I wanted to remember his face myself. I've packed that painting away somewhere and haven't looked at it in quite some time." Matt thought her eyes looked filled with sadness. "Perhaps I still have it somewhere."

"Gracious, Grandmother, why did you pack it away?"

Again, Lyonore remained quiet for several seconds. "It had become too painful for me to look at it," she replied softly, speaking as much to herself as to Matt. "Listen, Mattie, if you can come back this evening, I'll have the small knife ready for you to use for the faces. And, I'll see if I can find the painting of your grandfather for you to study. I think I remember where I probably put it."

"Grandmother, I'll come this evening."

Using a slender piece of charcoal, Matt practiced tracing the outlines of a few of the zodiac figures on a small slat his grandmother had provided. The boy worked slowly and carefully, he soon succeeded in re-producing reasonable likenesses on the surface of the wood.

"That's quite good, Matt," she said, offering him encouragement. "I think you're a natural."

"Well, I'll have to get better before I try it on the tray. But I think I might be able to do it."

"I think so, too," she said. "I'm pleased by how well you're doing already, never having done this before."

"Grandmother, weren't you going to tell me about my grandfather?"

"Was I? Well . . ."

"Oh, please do. I know so very little about him. Except that everyone says he's famous."

CHAPTER 24

Merlyn was perplexed. Where had his dreams gone, his visions? They'd *vanished*—dried up entirely. Occasionally, he'd gone a few days without having any consequential dreams, but never more than a week. His dreams provided him with clues to what was happening in the wider world; he relied on them. Now, imprisoned within this small space carved into the hillside, he needed them more than ever. Interpreting his dreams usually proved a bit challenging, but in the end, he could usually make some sense of them, even when he couldn't decipher them totally. Now—*nothing*.

Had the King returned to Britain's shores? Merlyn didn't know. Had Lute been able to track down Sir Pelleas? Was he now acting in concert with Pelleas and Nimuë? Would the three of them be able to thwart the evil designs of Mordred and Margause? He didn't know. The absence of his dreams, he feared, was auspicious.

Merlyn thought wistfully of Lute. He had always loved the young man. Merlyn had played a key role in the lad's begetting—it was Merlyn who had brought Arthur and Lyonore together—and Merlyn had always kept a close eye on the lad while he was growing up. Merlyn had stayed a safe distance away, and neither Lute nor Lyonore had been aware of it.

It was Merlyn who had talked the young man into going to Uther's grand city to see if his fate lay there. Merlyn had always had high hopes for the lad. He'd even tried hard to arrange things so that Lute could prove himself a worthy successor to King Arthur. In that matter Merlyn hadn't succeeded, though he still believed that the matter hadn't been finally resolved.

Yes, Merlyn missed Lute. And suddenly he was struck with the thought that his affection for Lute might even surpass his affection for Arthur. Merlyn had risked everything for Arthur—including the future of his own immortal soul, when he had arranged for Arthur's begetting by Uther and Igraine. He had also orchestrated that ill-fated attempted to dispose of the little boys born around the First of May. Then later he arranged the amorous rendezvous between Arthur and Lyonore. Unintentionally, he had placed Lute in great jeopardy by sending him to the city, not knowing that Mordred that had survived and had also gone to the city. Merlyn was as responsible for everything concerning Lute as he was for everything concerning Arthur.

Merlyn smiled at the realization that he also missed Raguel—that devilish and enigmatic brute. What a pair the two of them had made. Raguel's animal cunning complemented Merlyn's own fiendish cunning remarkably. And like Merlyn, Rags was a beast with a puckish sense of humor. Most unusual, Merlyn thought. And then we must add Tom into the mix. Raguel, Merlyn, and Tom—what a mischievous trio. Merlyn chuckled at the thought. Oh, how he wished he could be with them now, with Lute, and Tom, and Raguel. And also—Nimuë.

The enchanting Nimuë. Her he missed as much as the others—her teasing; their matching of wits; and the amorous desires she aroused in him whenever she was near. Strangely, he hadn't even dreamed of her lovely, delicate face, and her lissom body.

❖

The men and horses from the *Matthias* were now safely ashore, though the old ship's sailing days were clearly over. And there was still no news of the missing ship. As the hours went by, hopes of its survival dwindled.

"Lute?" said Sir Gomber. "I remember him. As young trainees, we were in the same fencing group."

"The King," said Sir Craddock, "seemed truly delighted when they said the fellow is coming with Sir Pelleas. What do you know of him?"

"Old Sir Ascomour, who as you know trained all the best of 'em—and that includes you 'n' me—always thought Lute was up there in the same class as Lamorak and Mordred. I don't know about that, but he was clearly the best of our group of eight."

"That's high praise, mentioning him in the same breath with those two. So, what happened to the fellow?"

"It's all rather a mystery. Right after he was knighted,

he just up and disappeared. Then a year or two later, we heard he'd become an earl at some god-forsaken place off in the hinterlands. Far as I know, he's never once returned to the city or to Arthur's court. Yes, Ascamour believed he had the makings of a Round Table knight, and yet the fellow just turned his back on the opportunity."

"Maybe he knew what he was doing. How many Round Table Knights do you reckon are still alive?"

"Only a meager handful, I guess," Sir Gomber said. "Well, maybe it's not too late for the likes of *me* to become one. And maybe it's not too late for Lute, if the fellow's had a change of heart."

It was after dusk when the scouts brought word of Mordred's arrival. Within an hour, their fires could be seen down below the hillside. Through the long night, no attempts were made by either group to make contact with the other.

The night was eerily still. A silvery moon tried to shed its light through a thick canopy of clouds. Occasional sounds from Mordred's camp drifted up to the men on the hilltop, men who tried, with minimal success, to get some sleep.

The dawn came slow and late beneath a gray, threatening sky. Before prime, a solitary rider emerged from the encircling encampment and trotted up the steep path toward the ancient hillfort. He halted before the outermost earthen bank and called out, "Come and speak!" Sir Ewen rode forth to meet him.

"Cousin," Ewen said to Agravaine, "well met, I hope."

"Probably not," Agravaine replied. "But the message I bring is that Mordred wishes to parley with our uncle, if he's amenable."

"I will find out," Ewen replied. "I suspect he will be."

"Beneath the large oak," Agravaine said, pointing to a huge tree down on the lower slopes of the hill. "In an hour. He can bring two others, no more." Agravaine turned his horse's head and trotted back to whence he'd come.

Arthur, Ewen, and Gawaine rode side by side. Mordred and two other men were waiting beneath the wide branches of the old oak tree. Atop the hill, the remainder of the King's knights sat mounted and fully armed. They had filed out slowly from behind the embankment and formed a long line, about sixty horsemen in all, ready to charge if the need arose. Far below them, Mordred's much larger cavalry had likewise formed ranks and were prepared to engage.

Arthur's troop of foot, consisting of bowmen and pikemen, remained out of sight behind the embankment. Should the horse soldiers below risk an uphill charge, they could be quickly maneuvered out front to repel the attack. Some of them hoped that Arthur could draw their foes into making such an unwise attack. Even though Mordred could be foolhardy, the chances of that occurring seemed small.

"Uncle," Mordred said, "greetings to you, sir. And to you as well, cousins," he said, with an acknowledging nod toward Gawaine and Ewen.

"I am your *brother*," Gawaine said, "not your cousin."

"So I have been told," Mordred replied sneeringly, wanting to get under Gawaine's skin.

"Hello, Mordred," the King said. "Come to provide us with an escort back to the city?"

"Uncle, in all candor, no. We haven't come for that purpose."

"Then what?"

"We've come to complete what Launcelot began. Knowing him, he was probably reluctant to finish the job, so we shall have to do it for him. *We* shan't be reluctant."

"Ha," scoffed Gawaine. "Launcelot wasn't *able* to finish the job. Nor will you be."

For a moment Mordred just glared at his half-brother.

"Are you open to negotiation?" Arthur asked.

"Yes . . . ," Mordred said, "but only on my terms."

"Never," muttered Gawaine.

"And what terms would these be?" Arthur asked.

"First of all, you must willingly relinquish the throne," Mordred said softly.

"Never!" Gawaine exclaimed.

"Also," Mordred went on, "at my Christmas coronation, you must be the one to place the mantle of kingship about my shoulders and anoint my head. I want Lute to be the one to place the crown upon my head."

"Only the bishop can anoint your head," Arthur said.

"This time we shall do it *my* way," Mordred replied.

"You can't make up your own rules," Ewen said.

"And who's going to stop me?"

"I am!" Gawaine spat out.

"*You?* You whose wounds are so obvious you can barely sit your horse? Brother, even if you were totally fit you could never stop me."

Gawain's hand fell to his side, and then his unsheathed weapon suddenly flashed in his hand.

"Do you draw on me?" Mordred said, surprised but pleased, his left hand now resting on the hilt of his own sword.

"Put up your sword!" Arthur demanded of Gawaine. With reluctance, the King's nephew slowly complied. "Mordred, your brother is in no condition to fight you or anyone else. If you possess an ounce of fairness you will refrain from accepting his challenge, despite what he may want."

"Since I am your own flesh and blood, father, I probably do possess an ounce of fairness—though I might have to search for it. Gawaine," he said, giving his brother a cold stare, "this time I shall spare you."

"Don't do me any favors, scum. I tell you now, Mordred, you shall never rule Britain."

"No? Well, in case you hadn't noticed, I rule Britain now. And I intend to make that permanent."

"Never," said Gawaine.

"Father," Mordred said, "will you do it? Will you place the mantle about my shoulders and anoint my head? Will you bestow your blessing on my kingship? And I also want Lute's. If so, Father, you shall live out your days with honor. You shall be given the honorific of being known as 'The Old King'."

❖

"You don't really mean all of that, do you?" Agravaine said to his brother as their horses trotted back to their encampment. "You are neither crazy nor stupid. My guess is you're just toying with him, giving him some shred of hope to cling to. Am I right?" Mordred just smiled and offered no reply, so Agravaine went on. "You can't let him return to the city alive, Mordred. If the people were to see him, there's no telling what might happen."

"Wouldn't it be a good thing to avoid all the killing that will occur if our forces engage?" Mordred said, finally responding to his brother's remarks. "Wouldn't it be simpler to take the fellow into our custody and then quietly dispatch and dispose of him along the way?"

"But what about his supporters? Don't we need to root out the most dangerous of them as well?"

"You sound a bit like Mother, Agravaine. But yes, various ones of them must certainly be swept away also— Gawaine and Ewen, of course, and Pelleas and Craddock; and if we ever get our hands on them, the traitorous bastards Bedivere and Kay. The others, I think, we needn't worry about too much. Once they see which way the wind is blowing, they'll quickly fall in line. Lute, though, is the one we must preserve. I'm serious about wanting him to place the crown upon my head—deadly serious." Agravaine couldn't help seeing the fire in his brother's eyes. When it came to Lute, his brother felt an internal fury he could barely contain.

"You can't do it, sire," Gawaine said, "you mustn't." The three of them had nearly reached the outer bank on the Knoll.

"You'll never reach the city alive, sire," Ewen said. "And even if you did, he means to do all he can to humiliate you."

"I agree," Arthur replied. "So, what do you propose we do?'

"We fight!" Gawaine said.

"No," Sir Ewen said, "We stall. We try to buy time and hope that Sir Pelleas and his knights get here soon."

"And how do we do that?" the king asked.

"Gawaine and I take him his answer in two hours. But you, sire, must remain behind with the men."

"And do we agree to his terms?"

"Yes . . . , but we request a few slight modifications."

"And if he doesn't agree?"

"He won't. But we try to persuade him. We can offer a few possible sweeteners. Try to get him to think about them."

"You have something in mind, Ewen?"

"My king, I do."

Sir Ewen had always been one of the quieter and less flamboyant of the king's handful of colorful nephews. Levelheaded and cautious, Ewen offered a contrast to the irrepressible personalities of Gawaine, Mordred, and Agravaine. In recent years, he had emerged as one of the king's most trusted counselors.

"That's good, Ewen," the king said. "Whatever it is you have in mind, I approve of it."

"I have something in mind, too, sire," Gawain said, fingering the hilt of his sword.

"That, nephew," Arthur said sternly, "shall be our plan of last resort."

❖

"We're getting close," Sir Pelleas said. "Probably another hour's ride."

"What do we intend to do?" Lute asked.

"We'll decide that once our scouts have apprised us of the situation. If there is an on-going battle, we must be prepared to charge into the midst of it and do all we can to support the King and his men."

"Sir, with respect," said Lute, "I suggest we select a specific target and concentrate our forces upon it."

"Yes, perhaps that might be possible. We certainly don't want to allow what strength we have to be so diluted as to be negligible."

Nimuë, riding apart from the two men and thinking her own thoughts, looked up at the sound of rapidly approaching hoofbeats. A solitary rider came rushing toward them on a large black stallion. It was Tom.

❖

Mordred, Agravaine, and Colgrevaunce waited on horseback beneath the great oak tree. They watched as Sir Ewen and Sir Gawaine approached.

"Arthur isn't with them," Colgrevaunce said, stating

what was already obvious to his companions.

"Well," Mordred said when the riders had halted their horses a few feet away, "has the fellow agreed to my terms?"

"Our *King*," Ewen replied, "mostly agrees."

"*Mostly?* Mostly isn't good enough. He must agree entirely. But out of curiosity, which part does he object to?"

"He's willing to hand over the kingship to you, and he's willing to place the mantle on your shoulders—"

"Good, good."

"But the bishop must be the one to anoint your head."

"You have to hand it to our purer-than-thou father, wanting the Church's approval."

"He also objects to having Lute participate."

"So, he wants to shield our little Lute from any possibility of being sullied. You and me, Gawaine, sad to say, we were sullied from the start. And the truth is, Lute was, too."

"Sullied?" grunted Gawaine. "What makes you say that?"

"When Arthur fathered me, brother, you know what he was doing—he was cuckolding your father."

"Mother was the one who seduced *him*."

"Oh, yes, Arthur was such a pure and innocent youth. Hah. Don't forget he'd already conceived Lute on some random slut."

"Mordred," Ewen asked, "are you acknowledging that Lute is your *elder* brother?" he was astonished by the admission.

"Sure, why not? It's not going to make any difference now. But Lute, unlike the three of us," he said, including Gawaine and Agravaine with a tilt of his head, has never been a true Pendragon. That benighted fellow is happier *not* being in line for the throne. At heart, Lute's nothing but a farmer. So, let's forget Lute. He's a nobody."

"Then his claim to the throne, Mordred, if he is the eldest son, is more valid than yours," Ewen said.

"Hardly, cousin. I'm the son of both a king *and* a queen. Lute is merely the son of some nameless whore."

"Brother, you take a more charitable view of our *queenly* mother than some folks do," said Gawaine scornfully.

Mordred glared at Gawaine. "Sirrah, are you insulting our mother?" Mordred's left hand reached across his body and gripped the hilt of his sword hanging at his right side.

"Our mother who has repeatedly defiled the legacy of our noble father?" Gawaine said. "I don't need to insult her, brother. She insults herself. And by embracing you, she insults herself even further. Our mother is more of a slut than Lute's mother will ever be."

"Draw, brother! Or I will kill you where you sit!"

"Wait!" shouted Sir Ewen. But it was too late.

CHAPTER 25

Mattie," the boy's grandmother said with delight, "You are a true artist. This is quite astonishing."

The boy couldn't help looking a little smug. "Yes, grandmother, I'm pleased with how it came out."

"I wonder where your artistic bent has come from? Not from your father, good as he is in so many things. Perhaps from your mother."

"Perhaps from you, Grandmother. Besides, you're the one who helped me with all the faces."

"I helped with only a few. You did most of them on your own, Matthew. It's a truly splendid piece. Your mother will be most pleased with her beautiful, clever Christmas gift. I'm a little jealous myself."

They stood together studying the wooden tray with its carvings of the signs of the zodiac around the raised edges.

"Matt, I recognize most of the faces. That man I don't, but I'm guessing he's one of the workers at the manor."

"Yes, that's Willykin."

"But Matt, who are these two?"

The boy looked down at the symbol for Gemini, the twins. Matt smiled. "Why, Grandmother, that one's *me*.

You don't recognize me? And that one's my friend Simon, Wat's grandson. We really aren't anything like twins. I'm a year older, and we don't look at all alike or like the same things. Simon likes learning, I like doing. I'd thought about making the second boy Johnny, Rob's son. Johnny and I are much more like brothers than Simon and I are. But then I thought that would be disloyal to Simon. Besides, I wanted the faces to be mostly of people my mother would know. She doesn't know Johnny."

"I like it that you are loyal to your friend," she said. "In that you are similar to your father."

Lyonore ran her eyes over all the faces, her inspection ending on the face for the sign of Leo. It was a face she knew Matt had never seen in real life, a face she herself hadn't seen in nearly thirty years. Matt had done a remarkable job in capturing a true likeness. Looking at it she felt a great surge of conflicting emotions. She had always wished the man well. Indeed, the truth was that she had never stopped loving him—despite the fact that he'd abandoned her long, long ago.

Merlyn sat up with a start. He'd felt a sudden shaking. Something was happening, something momentous. The shaking he'd felt wasn't an actual shaking, he realized. It was something he'd sensed with his second sight rather than something that had occurred in the physical world. But he had no doubt that somewhere, far off, something was unfolding, some event of great consequence. It could only involve the King, he believed. Merlyn had always agreed with the ancient belief that the king and the land were one, that the two were inextricably bound together. If all was well with the king, all was well with the land, and vice versa. Now, something was happening that involved the king. His well-being—and that of the land—were at stake.

Merlyn climbed to his feet and stepped over to where the opening to his hillside abode was blocked by an invisible wall. His vision was unimpeded, but all he could see were trees and hills. All he could hear were the sounds of the river and the songs of the birds. All looked normal. But somewhere, far off, all was not normal.

A vision of of Nimuë suddenly entered his head. He could see her, dashing along on a sleek bay horse, her long, black braid flowing freely behind her, a look of fierce determination on her face. Nimuë was a warrior-woman going into battle. Merlyn suddenly smiled. Nimuë was armed with knowledge he had shared with her and skills he had helped her develop. She was his surrogate. Except, he thought with a wintry smile, she was even better than he was. He would have failed; *she* would not. She would prevail.

Were Tom and Lute there, too? He didn't know. But he felt certain of one thing: the massive black stallion named Raguel *was* there—for better or for worse.

❖

"They've engaged!" the scout shouted out, his mount still fifty yards away.

"Then we must ride!" one of the captains declared.

The riders in the vanguard began spurring their horses.

"Stop!" Sir Pelleas shouted. "You must stop! We have to know the positions."

"Sir, the battle is already going on," the scout shouted back. "It's being fought on the seaward side of the Knoll. The King's knights have come down from their positions on the higher slopes and engaged with Mordred's cavalry."

Sir Pelleas shouted back, "Is that where we should concentrate our attack? We need to be certain!"

"I'll go 'n' check things out," Tom said. "Get your fellas as close to the Knoll as you dare. I'll be back to tell you in half an hour. I can get closer to the Knoll than your scouts can."

"Good lad, Tom," Lute said, nodding his agreement.

Raguel whinnied, and Tom gave Lute an upward thumb. Then they were off.

Lute, now in his late twenties, had kept himself very fit, mostly through his own vigorous labors on and about the manor, as well as by his long daily rides, when he was often accompanied by Jill. Back in the six-month period when he was in the city training for knighthood, he'd had a good many physical confrontations of one sort or another, but that was a decade ago. Twice in his life Lute's actions toward a foe had had fatal consequences. Both of those events had grieved him greatly, despite his knowing that in each case he was defending himself and in each case the man had fully deserved what he got.

Lute's last physical confrontation with a foe had *nearly*

proved fatal. That was the drastic encounter that occurred shortly after Lute had suddenly decided he would bid adieu to the city—an encounter in which Mordred, after slinking after Lute, had set upon him unawares in a meadow. At the time, Lute thought he'd killed his half-brother, right after Mordred had very nearly killed him. Lute had left Mordred lying there for dead in the meadow, and even the sharp-eyed Tom when he'd checked Mordred out, was convinced the fellow was dead. But he wasn't; by some miracle, he'd survived. Lute believed the world would be a better place with Mordred gone from it. But even so, as villainous and vile as Mordred was, killing him was not something Lute would ever have chosen to do.

During the ensuing decade, while Lute lived his quiet life as the Earl of Sanham, he'd tried as best he could to maintain his fencing skills. From the very beginning of his training days with Sir Ascomour back in the city, Lute had proved adept, and the weapons-master had quickly seen Lute as an extremely promising pupil. Perhaps the lad hadn't possessed all of Mordred's natural gifts, but he'd had quick reflexes, fierce determination, and a talent for sizing up an opponent and capitalizing on that opponent's chief weakness. Also to his credit, Lute was a calm, intelligent fencer, whereas Mordred, despite his remarkable talents, had always been impatient and arrogant.

Over the past two years, Lute had been working with Neely, first teaching the lad the rudiments of the sport and then more advanced techniques; just as Neely had quickly become good at chess, he'd soon mastered the basics of fencing. In fact, he'd become good enough to push Lute to the limit a few times, though unlike their chess matches, Lute had never intentionally let Neely best him in a fencing match. To Lute, doing that would have compromised the ethical principles of the noble sport.

Now, riding toward what might prove to be a final, fatal combat, Lute's nerves were all a-jangle. Did he want to employ the skills he'd once worked so assiduously to achieve? Did he still *have* them? Or was he deluding himself, engaging in a fool's errand? He didn't know. But there was one thing he did know—he must do whatever he could to aid King Arthur, his father, in his time of need.

❖

"Draw, brother!" shouted the infuriated Sir Gawaine. "Draw! Or I will kill you where you sit!"

Emblazoned on Mordred's black shield was a silver falcon, its talons flaring. On Gawaine's shield, a golden five-pointed star shone brightly against a field of red. Their steeds wore trappings to match. The half-brothers were a pair of proud, vain men—and they *hated* each other.

Sir Gawaine was at a distinct disadvantage. He'd been injured twice in his recent encounters with Sir Launcelot across the water, and his severe head wounds were still but partially healed. But Gawaine was a powerful, strong-willed man, and a most able warrior. He could wield a sword with the best of them, and he rode upon Gringolet, one of the finest steeds in the kingdom.

But Mordred *was* the best of them. He was the young man who'd completed his training for knighthood faster than anyone else ever had; and he was the youngest man ever inducted into the Fellowship of the Round Table knights; furthermore, he was the one who had taken down the great rebel, King Rience, single-handedly. With a little help from Sir Agravaine, he had killed the formidable Sir Lamorak. And, he had also nearly killed Tom and also Lute. It was only because of Merlyn's timely assistance and skillful aid—and Raguel's—that they'd survived.

Now Mordred's chance to wreak havoc on his hated half-brother and his hated father had finally come. It would be Gawaine first, then it would be Arthur. Mordred was beside himself with glee.

In almost no time at all, Mordred's men formed a wide circle about the pair of fighters. They gave them plenty of space for the fatal encounter while making sure that Gawaine would be on his own versus Mordred, that he would receive no assistance from Sir Ewen or anyone else.

As Sir Pelleas and his knights skirted the western flank of the Knoll, half a mile before them they saw Mordred's amassed forces. As they neared, a mighty roar of delight went up.

"He's done it!" a voice rang out.

"No one ever doubted that he would," exclaimed another loud voice.

"Look! Here comes some more fun!" someone else shouted.

Now alerted to the rapid approach of their foe, Mordred's knights swung about to face the on-coming riders. Upon Sir Agravaine's shouted commands, the knights quickly formed a pair of battle lines, one before the other. Sir Colgrevaunce was positioned at the center of the first line. As Sir Pelleas's troupe drew nearer, they charged. Pelleas, however, chose to decline the engagement. With precision, his line of knights wheeled to the right, and Colgrevaunce's riders charged after them in hot pursuit.

Once the two lines of Mordred's force were separated by a good distance, Pelleas's knights suddenly reversed course. Wheeling about quickly, they prepared to engage in battle. A ferocious and bloody melee soon erupted. Agravaine's second line came up quickly, but before they could enter the fray, King Arthur and his knights came roaring down from the higher slopes of the Knoll and set upon them. It was a battle royal.

Tom, on Raguel, led Lute and Nimuë up a narrow defile formed by a natural fold in the topography. They were on the eastern side of the Knoll, the side away from the battle, but the battle sounds from the western side were quite audible.

"Hurry!" Tom shouted. Fortunately, Lute and Nimuë's mounts were nearly able to match Raguel's quick pace. When they reached the outer encircling earthwork, there was no one there to challenge them. Indeed, the ring fort atop the Knoll was now completely deserted. Arthur and his men had abandoned it to go down and join the battle.

For a moment, the two men and the woman stood

there atop the Knoll observing the seething, chaotic mass of horses and warriors beneath them. The stertorous breathing of their mounts were accompanied by the battle sounds coming from below.

The battle seemed to have become totally haphazard. Both Arthur's troupe and Sir Pelleas's smaller forces were thoroughly commingled with Mordred's. Men and horses screamed and fell. The lower slopes of the Knoll were fast becoming a charnel house of blood and gore. Mordred's advantage in numbers had declined, and on the field of battle only a few riders remained unhorsed. Men were fighting all across the area, weapon to weapon and hand to hand.

Gradually, a picture came into focus. Now just two small clutches of men were all that remained afoot. The smaller of the two, maybe eight men in all, had formed about King Arthur, while the slightly larger group contained Mordred and Agravaine. Lute could see that Mordred's group was advancing slowly toward King Arthur and his last few defenders. Lute saw no sign of Sir Pelleas.

"I must go to him," Lute said softly, as much to himself as to his companions.

"Okay if me 'n' Raguel try 'n' ride roughshod over Mordred and his pals?" Tom asked.

"Do it!" Nimuë spat out. "And I will join you in doing it."

"I'll be with the King," Lute said.

"Yes," Nimuë replied. "We'll join you when we can."

Chapter 26

King Arthur and Mordred stood facing each other, Mordred holding his bloody sword in his raised left hand. Arthur clutched a ten-foot pike in both hands, its steel-enclosed head laying in the dirt a few feet in front of Mordred.

Mordred was entirely on his own now, his final defenders having abandoned him in terror when a monstrous black stallion had come crashing upon them. That beast, it had seemed to them, was a creature not of this world. It was like some fire-breathing monstrosity sent by the very Devil himself. Perched upon the demon's back was a grinning, devilish little imp wielding a glowing falchion; with him, a wild-haired harridan who was hurling the vilest of imprecations at them. They'd fled, the devilish creatures pursuing them.

But Mordred, intent upon Arthur, was imperious to the threat of the rider on the black horse and his female companion. Mordred hadn't fled. Now he stood just a few feet in front of the King.

Arthur, his body consumed by exhaustion and his mind filled with black despair, didn't speak. Sir Ewen lay dead at his feet. Sir Gawaine, his beloved nephew, lay dead a hundred yards away. Now his son, the man to whom he had entrusted his kingdom, meant to consummate his evil deeds by killing him. Arthur prayed to be able to summon up the strength for one final act.

It was then that another horseman suddenly appeared on the scene. It was Lute. Kicking his feet free of his stirrups, Lute leapt from his saddle. In no more than a second or two he'd interposed himself between his father and his brother. He raised his weapon.

Mordred stared at Lute. Neither man spoke.

"Put down your sword, Mordred," Lute said, finally. "Look around you. It's hopeless. It's all finished."

"No, Lute. It isn't finished. Not until you and our father are both dead."

"Then maybe, brother, you had best start with me."

"Maybe I had."

To Tom, sitting on Raguel fifty yards away, it looked to be a fairly even fight. The two men slowly circled each other, feinting and thrusting. Mordred was clearly the more able swordsman, his fencing skills honed by his months of training against the finest fencers in the kingdom. Lute, who'd only had Neely's rudimentary efforts to help him retain his skills, was none the less much fresher, not having already spent an hour in the fray.

King Arthur looked on helplessly as his two sons

engaged in their final, fateful struggle. For the first five minutes Lute defended himself adroitly; and he even managed to land the first significant blow, with a quick backhand slash slicing the little finger from Mordred's right hand. The wound infuriated Mordred, but he didn't lose his composure, and soon his greater skill began to make all the difference. First he landed a wicked blow to Lute's exposed left forearm; and then, using brute force rather than subtlety, he forced Lute backward. Unaware of the inert body of Sir Ewen, Lute tripped, then stumbled. He landed hard on his back, his head smacking against the packed earth. He was momentarily stunned. Violating the basic rules of chivalry by stabbing a downed man, Mordred thrust his blade into Lute's thigh at a place where his mail shirt offered him no protection.

With Lute down and out, Mordred turned his attention to the King.

"Father," he whispered, just loud enough for Arthur to hear him, "the time has come. Your days . . . *sire*," he said scornfully, "are over."

As Mordred slithered forward, Arthur suddenly raised the tip end of the pike. With all the strength he could muster, he thrust the weapon straight into the center of Mordred's torso. The steel head of the pike pierced Mordred's mail shirt and passed through him. It extended half a foot out of Mordred's back.

From the throat of the younger man came a ghastly sound. Blood began to pour from his chest wound and then from his mouth. For a moment, it was as if time stood still. Arthur, as a result of his effort, seemed totally spent. But Mordred wasn't quite finished. Now his body was moving again, his body fueled by massive amounts of adrenaline—as well as by hate. Because of the adrenaline, Mordred felt little pain and had almost superhuman strength. By force of will, he inched himself forward, slowly working his way up the length of the pike's long handle; slowly it passed through his torso as he moved. His eyes were dimming as he neared his father; his lips bore a faint smile.

"Now!" came his soft exclamation as he brought down his blade with a final smite upon King Arthur's helmet. The King toppled to the ground, senseless. For a second Mordred's body swayed; then he too went down. Mordred had collapsed atop the body of his fallen father.

Chapter 27

The chilly December afternoon was drawing on. It would be dark in another hour.

"How's it lookin'?" Tom asked Nimuë.

"Not so good," came her soft reply. She had rolled Mordred's corpse off of the King and was crouched down over Arthur's body.

"Lute's not so good, neither," Tom said. "Least I got his blood all stopped up. But lord-a-mercy, he's got a lump a-back o' his head size of a hen's egg. Musta whacked it 'gainst a rock or sumpthin' when he went down. Still a-breathin', though."

"The King is breathing also. Let's see if we can't get the both of 'em up to the hillfort. That's where all their supplies will be."

Emerging from the murk came two men on horseback. They were Sir Craddock and Sir Sagramour.

"So, you blokes made it, eh?" Tom asked. "That's good, 'cuz we surely can use ya now."

The two knights carefully lifted Arthur and Lute and

draped them over the backs of their mounts.

"Follow me," said Nimuë. She and the pair of knights began to move upward toward the hillfort on top of Brent Knoll. Tom remained behind.

"I'll be with yas soon's I track down Raguel," he said.

Once the others had gone some distance up the steep hill, Tom stepped over to Mordred's fallen body. He looked down at the corpse of this man whom he so greatly despised. He studied Mordred closely. This time Tom wouldn't make the mistake he'd made a decade earlier. This time he would be absolutely sure the dastardly fellow was dead. Tom had real qualms about mutilating dead bodies. It was a vile practice. This time, too, he wouldn't do it. But what he would do, and did do, was run his sharp blade firmly, deeply across Mordred's throat. When no fresh blood seeped from the wound, Tom felt certain the bastard was dead.

Just to be doubly sure, though, Tom lifted Mordred's right wrist and felt for a pulse. No pulse. Then he noticed the fingers. One of them, the smallest one, was missing. Goodness sakes, Lute must've lopped it off during their fight. The notion that Lute had inflicted some pain on this horrible man before he'd died brought a smile to Tom's lips. He scanned the ground over which the two men had had their fateful fight. What had happened to that missing finger?

"Ah," he said at last. He spotted a little trail of blood and followed it with his eye. The trail led him straight to the detached digit. Yes, there was the small, bloody finger, lying half covered with dirt. Tom bent down and picked it up. Would you look at that! There was a ring on it. Tom knew the ring. He'd seen it a decade ago. Then, it had required all his strength of will not to take it from Mordred's body. Then, he'd been sorely tempted to, but his conscience, feeble as his conscience had always been, had somehow prevented him from doing so.

Tom worked the ring off of the finger. He stared at the small naked finger for a moment, then dropped the stinkin' thing back down into the dirt. It would make a tempting morsel for a scavenging crow.

Tom held the ring up to his eye and studied it. Though the daylight was mostly gone now, Tom could still see the inscription on the inside of the ring. He recognized the words as being Latin, but he wasn't familiar enough with the language to be able to read it. Nevertheless, speaking aloud, Tom offered his own inventive translation. "What does it say? you ask—'Today, my luck ran out'."

Tom rolled the ring around in the palm of his hand. It was heavy. No doubt it was gold. No doubt it was a very valuable object. There was no doubt, too, that Tom wanted nothing to do with the stinkin' thing.

Cocking his arm, he flung the ring as far as he could, off into the darkness.

Inside the hillfort, the two knights had set a fire to burning. Nimuë had draped cloaks over Arthur and Lute, who now lay stretched out nearby. Arthur lay quietly but Lute had begun to show signs of life. When he struggled to sit up, Nimuë placed her hand on his shoulder and said softly, "No, no, not just yet. Soon, though." Lute offered an audible groan in reply but lay back down as she wanted him to.

After a few minutes, Tom arrived with Raguel and Nimuë's palfrey. "I found Lute's horse, too, all safe 'n' sound," he said. "But Arthur's I had to put down. He were so badly gored, his guts was all a-hangin' out."

"Ya think any of our knights might still be alive?" Sir Craddock asked.

Tom shook his head. "Some o' Mordred's might be. Heard several of 'em a-moanin'. But I ain't about ta give them bastards no help. Them bastards have reaped what they sowed."

"I'll go out tonight and have a good look," said Sir Sagramour. "I'll assist any of the severely wounded."

"Assist?" asked Tom.

"Yes, assist," replied the stony-faced Sir Sagramour.

They ate hunks of hard bread and a hot and steamy broth Nimuë had somehow managed to concoct. She'd stirred in various dried herbs from her pack, herbs which gave the broth a tangy, pungent flavor.

"What was all them powders ya put in there?" Tom asked. "Kinda gives it a bit of a bite."

"Just eat," she replied.

"Reminds me a lot of sumpthin' old Merlyn once cooked up for me."

She smiled at Tom's remark. "Just eat," she said again,

picturing in her mind Merlyn all by himself in his hillside abode, his jars of herbs and spices on a rock shelf behind him. It was a bittersweet thought.

They managed to prop up Lute, who had now returned to full consciousness. He was able to hold his own bowl of the broth and slurp down most of it.

"You're the fellow who fought that last fight with Mordred?" Sir Craddock asked him.

Lute nodded.

"That was some fight. I was trying to get to the King myself when I saw you step in. A brave thing to do, taking on Mordred like that. Who are you, anyway?"

"I'm Lute."

"He's the Earl of Sanham," Tom added quickly. He thought about saying more, but the look in Lute's eye told him not to.

"And I'm Nimuë," the woman said. "You are Sir Sagramour and Sir Craddock, right? Pelleas told me about you."

"Sir Pelleas? Has he survived the fight?" Sagramour asked.

"Alas," she said, "he and Sir Ewen were the last two to fall protecting the King."

"If Sir Pelleas hadn't come with his small troupe of loyal men," Sir Sagramour said, "Mordred would certainly have triumphed. Pelleas was a valiant fellow."

"One of the best," Sir Craddock added.

For a lengthy spell they all remained quiet. Then Sir Craddock asked, "So, what do we do now?"

It was Nimuë who replied. "We need a boat," she said.

"A boat? What for?"

"To get us to Ynys Rhonech. We must take the King there. The nuns have a superb herb garden, one of the finest there is. I must have access to it. The island isn't far. It shouldn't take us more than an hour or two to sail there."

"That would depend on the winds and the currents," Sir Craddock said, "but yes, I think it shouldn't be too hard. I've been there once myself."

"Sorry to say," Nimuë went on, "I think it's the King's only chance."

The two knights stared at her. Could they entrust the King to her? Did she really know what she was doing? It appeared they had little choice.

"There's a couple of ships anchored just off the beach at Burnham Sands," Sir Sagramour said, "and maybe a smaller boat or two. One of them might suit your purposes. We could probably work them, right?" he said, looking at Sir Craddock.

"No doubt we could," he replied.

"I could help," Lute said. "That hot broth has really set me up."

"No," Nimuë said. "You must come with us, but you must not exert yourself too much. That's a serious wound in your leg. You must stay off it."

"While you folks're foolin' with sailin' to that island, I'll attend to the horses. Get 'em all back to the city for yas, yeah?" Tom said.

"You could do that?" Craddock asked. "Handle all those horses by yourself?"

Tom just laughed. "Oh, it'll only be five or six of 'em, not no big hardship. I been handlin' multiple horses ever since I were a tiny tike."

"And perhaps we'd better not go into detail about just *how* he's been handling all those horses," Lute said. He was grinning.

"Why, sir, you surely ain't implyin' that I've had any iillegal or llegitimate dealings with horses, are ya?"

"Of course not, Tom," Lute said. "I would never do such a thing."

"That's not quite what Merlyn says about you, Tom," Nimuë added.

After a short pause Tom's said. "That old feller? Why hell's bells, that old feller don't know all he thinks he knows."

Nimuë laughed. "I don't disagree with you there," she said. "No, he certainly doesn't."

Sir Cradock and Sir Sagramour exchanged more glances. Who *were* these strange people?

The knights built up the fire for the long, cold night, and Nimuë tended to Arthur's and Lute's wounds one last time before retiring herself. Only then did she realize how truly exhausted she was. Tom fed and watered the horses, then bedded down also.

It was in the middle of the moonlit night that the two knights roused themselves and wandered down to the field of battle. They were gone for about two hours, but neither Tom nor Nimuë was aware of their activities. Both of them slept beneath their thick cloaks like two small bears hibernating in the winter. They were so deeply asleep they didn't realize that after the return of the two knights, no more moans or groans came from the hillside down below.

Chapter 28

The city was awash with rumors: . . . the King was alive and well and on his way back; . . . the King was dead, killed by Mordred, and the Prince Regent would be crowned at Christmas; . . . the Prince Regent and all his men were dead, Mordred killed by the King himself; . . . the King was dead, killed by Launcelot during their encounter across the water . . . the King was dead, but he had a second son, who would succeed him as king; . . and others. The truth was, no one was certain of anything.

Most of these rumors meant little to Simon. The boy remained secluded at the chandler's shop on the city's lowest level where he had quickly settled in and become an extra set of hands for Mary's father. Being a quick learner, Simon was soon earning his daily fare. Mary doted on the boy, and her father entrusted him with many of the shop's more basic tasks.

Simon's favorite among his new friends, though, was the woman named Magdalene. She visited most days, and he was disappointed on the days when she didn't. She usually brought choice bits of news or gossip from the castle and sometimes messages from Yonec. The woman showed a keen interest in Simon's life in Sanham with his grandfather, a subject Simon was happy to discuss with her.

One day she asked him, "Simon, have you ever come across a man in Sanham whose name is Brogan?"

Simon looked up from the candle mold into which he was pouring hot wax. "Brogan? Why, yes, I know the fellow you mean. Not real well, but a little bit."

"What can you tell me about him?"

"He's a rather quiet fellow, but tall and strong. Some folks think that since he don't talk so much, he can't be too bright. Them folks is wrong. My grandfather says Brogan's steady as a rock, and loyal to the earl as the day is long."

"Sounds like your grandfather admires him, Simon."

"I s'pose he does. I never thought much about it."

"I've seen him only a few times," Magdalene said, "but I very much hope to see him again."

"You'd probably have to go to Sanham in order to do that. Don't think he's much of a city fellow." She nodded.

"I'm not really sure what I am," Simon went on. "I miss my grandfather, but I've sure come to love the city."

"What do you especially love about it? The castle? The fountains? The high walls? All the activity?"

"Not the castle," Simon said, "definitely not the castle. No, I think my favorite place is the minster. I really liked learning from Father Urias. Hope I can get back ta doin' that sometime. Most of all, I love seeing all the wondrous books they have there."

"Simon!" came the loud voice of the chandler. "Where's them rush lights you was preparin' for me?"

"Comin', sir," the boy shouted back. "Got 'em all ready for you."

Magdalene slipped quietly out the rear door of the chandler's shop. "Yes," she thought, "I just might have to go to Sanham. I wonder how I could do that."

❖

Lyonore tied the thick twine around the old blanket in which she'd wrapped Matt's wooden tray. His project, entirely his own idea and mostly the product of his own labors, had turned out really well. The boy was justifiably proud of it. Lyonore imagined the look of delight on Jillian's face when she opened it.

The Feast of the Nativity was now just a week away, and Neely would be leaving for Sanham in the morning. With all the uncertainty in the world—even in the tiny hamlet of Northering they'd heard many of the rumors— she worried about the young man's safety, traveling alone.

Matthew's project had revived in the woman thoughts of the King, thoughts she had tried to suppress for nearly three decades. She very much hoped the rumors of the King's death were not true. Now she had to admit to herself that all this time she'd secretly harbored the hope that one day the two of them would meet again. As the years had slipped past, though, that possibility had seemed more and more unlikely. She now understood, from what

Lute had told her, that the King *had* tried to find her way back then, before he'd concluded that she didn't wish to be found. It had been about two years later, the year after Lute had been born, when word came that the King had taken a wife, a wife everyone said was the most beautiful woman in the whole kingdom.

That news had hurt Lyonore very much. But she knew she shared one thing with the King that over the years had been denied to the queen—a son. Man and wife are one flesh, the Church teaches, but she felt herself to be more one flesh with the King than the woman who was his wife because Lyonore and the King had come together to *create* one flesh. That was a fact that could never be taken away from her. It was a fact she cherished.

❖

At the manor house in Sanham, life went on much as usual. Folks there had heard all the rumors, too, but it was only Jillian and Brogan who found them disquieting. Old Wat, desperate for news of Simon, couldn't have cared less about what had happened, or hadn't happened, to the Prince Regent. He did care about Lute, but he knew Lute could look after himself. His grandson Simon, though, way off in the city like that, was just a babe in the woods.

The rumor that was especially disconcerting to Jill was the suggestion that Mordred wasn't the King's only son, that he'd had a second son people hadn't known about, and that this man might soon become the newly crowned king. She knew that Lute had never wished it to be known that he was the King's son, nor did he have any real desire to be king. But she also knew that if he thought he had to do it for the sake of the kingdom, he would.

Absent from all the rumors was any mention of the Queen. Jill found that puzzling. What had happened to this woman who had been at the center of all the turmoil at court? Jill had heard that it had been Launcelot's fatal attraction to the Queen which had led to the tearing apart of entire Fellowship of the Round Table.

Jillian didn't ascribe blame to the Queen, or to Launcelot, or to the King. She didn't know enough about the complex events that had transpired to do that. The only one whose actions she felt she knew enough about to judge was Mordred. That man, she believed, was nothing but a vile, black-hearted villain.

Fatal attraction was something Merlyn knew a good bit about. Once, long ago, he had aided King Uther in satisfying his uncontrollable lust for Igraine. His actions had led directly to the birth of Arthur, a result Merlyn had relished. Then, later, Merlyn had done much the same for Arthur when the lad became infatuated with Lyonore. That attraction had led to the birth of Lute. In more recent times, Merlyn had pursued his own ill-fated desires for a woman. His obsession with Nimuë had spawned his present predicament, one in which he was likely to remain until the end of time. Merlyn knew it was poetic justice that he, too, had been ensnared by lust, which meant that he would probably spend the rest of his days in this little cave he'd fashioned with his own hands.

The earth-shaking events Merlyn had felt certain were occurring now seemed to have subsided. He knew they must have reached a conclusion of some sort. Merlyn believed that the entire situation must be moving slowly, inexorably, toward its inevitable conclusion, whatever that might turn out to be. At the center of it, surely, were the King and Lute and Nimuë. Merlyn firmly believed that all three of them were still alive. He couldn't admit to any other possibilities. He also believed that Tom and Raguel were alive and had done all they could to aid Lute and Arthur.

Merlyn smiled. What a strange crew the four of us are, he thought—a stray waif, a demonic horse, a terrifyingly beautiful and intelligent witch-woman, and himself, whatever *he* was. Thank goodness for Arthur and Lute, he thought, two semi-normal human beings for whose existence he bore much responsibility.

Tom left the five horses and a small pouch filled with silver coins in the keeping of his farmer friend just outside the city. The man hefted the coins and clinked them together inside the pouch. They would do nicely. They would even make up for the fact that the huge black stallion he'd be keeping gave him, and all his other horses, the heebie-jeebies.

"Can't say how long they'll need ta be here," Tom said. "Least a couple o' days. But I'll come back to check on 'em sooner'n that."

"Along with a few additional coins?"

Tom gave the fellow a fierce stare. "Does I look like I's made o' money?"

His friend laughed. He shook the pouch with the coins. "Nah, you're good for at least a week."

Half an hour later, Tom stood with some others before the long bridge that led into the city's great gateway. Now through the massive portal came a coach and four and the entourage of whoever was in the coach. Four mounted riders preceded the coach, and another six rode behind. As the coach rumbled by, Tom could see two heads inside. They belonged to Queen Margause of Lothian and the Duke of Ortwick, a man who had once been an intimate associate of King Lot of Lothian, Margause's deceased husband.

"Looks like rats from a sinking ship," muttered a fellow standing nearby.

"Oh? Why's that?" Tom asked him.

"The Prince Regent's gone now. Maybe gone in more ways than one. Leastways, these folks're thinkin' they'd best get while the gettin's good."

"The Prince Regent is gone, eh?" Tom said. "Well, I like the sound of that." Tom knew for a fact that the Prince Regent *was* gone. He himself had made very damn certain of it.

CHAPTER 29

The inlet, a mere cleft amidst the high cliffs, suddenly appeared, and Sir Craddock skillfully guided their small craft through the narrow opening. Ynys Rhonech was a rugged little islet, entirely ringed by steep, rocky escarpments. It was obviously home to a myriad of seabirds. It was home also to a small monastic community of women.

Nimuë leapt over the side along with the two knights. The tide was out, and together they pulled the boat up to a safe position high on the shingle beach. Their arrival was no secret. For the last half hour, women had been observing their approach. Now a pair of them, in nuns' garb, waited at the foot of the curving path that ascended toward the monastic enclosure.

"Holy Mother," Nimuë said, dipping her head to the short, stout nun on whose breast hung a pectoral cross, "we have brought a severely wounded man who needs immediate attention. I may be able to save him, if you could find space for him in your infirmary and kindly allow me access to your renown herb garden."

The younger of the two women frowned at Nimuë. The older woman brought one hand to her chin and looked at Nimuë thoughtfully. "Do we know you?" she asked.

"We *do*," her younger companion said softly.

"It's possible," Nimuë admitted. "I once trained for my novitiate. Not here, but in a sister house to yours."

"You are *Nimuë*," the younger woman said, her words dripping with scorn. "*We* know of you." The older woman placed her hand on the younger one's arm to calm her.

"Who is it you have brought here?" she asked.

"Three knights of the Round Table and their king."

"King *Arthur?* Is *he* the wounded man?"

"Indeed, Holy Mother, he is."

"Sister Martha, go back and prepare a chamber for him."

"Are you going to allow *her* to set foot inside our holy precinct?"

"Sister Martha! Do as I have instructed you to do." Nimuë had to suppress a smile at the sharp rebuke. "Please wait here for ten minutes," she said to Nimuë, "then bring the King. Once we have made him comfortable, I'll take you to the herb garden."

"Will you allow me to consult the herbalist?"

"Of course. Though, truthfully, I am as knowledgeable as she is. I was the one who trained her."

"You are Sister Eloise?"

"I am."

"I have heard many good things spoken of you."

The woman blushed. "All greatly exaggerated, no

doubt. Well, the accommodations we can provide for you will be quite modest, I'm afraid, but we'll do our best to make you comfortable."

Three women walked along the narrow paths between the small plots of herbs and flowers in the garden. They were Nimuë, Sister Eloise, and a round-shaped, round-faced nun with a cheerful mien. She was the herbalist and her name was Sister Blanche. As she spoke the common name of each plant, Nimuë immediately provided the Latin name. It was almost like an antiphonal chant: "milk thistle"—"silybum marianum"; "lemon balm"—"melissa officinalis;" "clary sage"—"salvia sclarea"; "betony"—"stachys officinalis." Sister Eloise smiled at the two women's little recitation.

Afterward, Nimuë followed Sister Blanche and Sister Eloise to the small room where the herbalist stored her dried herbs and steeped her infusions. On her shelves lay an array of small ceramic pots and lidded jars, all clearly labeled.

"Would it be possible for me to have some small amounts of several of your herbs?"

"Of course," replied Sister Blanche, "pretty much anything you wish, though with a few exceptions."

"To begin with, I would like to have some St. John's wort and some comfrey. Oh, and of course chamomile."

"Oh, yes, all of them are right there in their jars, as you can see from the labels. But do be careful with the comfrey, will you?"

"I'm well aware of the dangers, Sister Blanche. After I give it further thought, I'll probably need a few more items."

"All you need do is ask."

"Well, let me ask you this, then. Have either of you, per chance," Nimuë asked, "ever prepared a salve known as The Three Marys' Ointment?"

The question caught the other two women off guard. They both looked rather aghast. For a moment they stared at each other before Sister Eloise finally spoke. "Where have you heard of that?" she asked.

"I've never actually *heard* of it. But I have read of it."

"Then surely you know that no one is ever permitted to make it. Even if the formula, now long lost, were known. Oh no, it would be a terrible sacrilege. That was created to be used but one time and for one purpose."

"Yes," Nimuë said softly, "and for the holiest of purposes. I do understand. And yet . . . ."

"Well, we shall consider the matter," Sister Eloise said.

Sister Blanche looked nearly bowled over by her mother superior's remark. "We shall?" she couldn't help blurting out. She obviously thought that it was entirely out of the question. But then the wisdom in Sister Eloise's decision dawned on her. The whole convent would consider the matter; and their final answer would be a resounding *no*.

❖

During their few days on Ynys Rhonech, Sir Craddock

and Sir Sagramour dined in the refectory with the nuns, and they joined the nuns in the evening for the service of compline. The whole time, however, Lute remained with his father in a small room inside the infirmary. The King still had not regained consciousness, but he'd responded well to the nuns' tender ministrations. Some color had returned to his cheeks, and his pulse was now stronger. Lute, too, was doing better. His thigh wound, left open to the air, had scabbed up well, and the sizeable lump on his head had nearly disappeared.

Sister Blanche had prepared for Nimuë small amounts of each of the plants she'd requested. But there was one particular plant Nimuë hadn't mentioned which she especially wanted. So, in the dark of their second night at the monastery, between lauds and matins, she slipped out alone into the monastery garden while the nuns were asleep or otherwise occupied alone in their cells, to search out that plant. She had noticed it on the first day as she walked the gardens with Sister Eloise and Sister Blanche, though she was careful not to pay it any attention. She hadn't asked for it because she knew the nuns wouldn't want her to have any of it. It was a plant called *Atropa Belladona*, a plant whose efficacy she had once discussed with Merlyn.

The next afternoon in the monastery cloisters, Sister Eloise and Nimuë walked companionably side by side. A genuinely warm feeling had developed between the women, though the feeling of the other nuns toward

Nimuë was anything but warm. They resented her presence, maybe even feared it, and wished her gone. They were about to get their wish.

"We'll be leaving in the morning," Nimuë said to Sister Eloise. The older woman nodded. She knew that it was for the best. She was sorry that Nimuë hadn't been able to get from them what she'd wanted, but at least they had helped ease the King's pain for a short time, and successfully tended to the wounds of the younger man.

"I am sorry you will be leaving so soon."

"The sisters are troubled by my presence, and also by that of the men."

"They are unused to having men about. It disconcerts them. But you, Nimuë, some of them have heard of you. They think that you are a non-believer, or even worse, a heretic."

"Do you think that, too?"

Sister Eloise hesitated before replying. "I think you are a very intelligent woman who is doing the best she can. I believe that your intentions are good. As for your beliefs, that is between you and God."

❖

A great many citizens had crowded into the city's lowest square. The news of the imminent arrival of two famous and much-loved knights had spread through the city like a wild fire. A festive mood prevailed. People sensed that the short, unhappy reign of the Prince Regent had come to an end, and they were more than ready for it to happen.

Then beneath the inner portcullis and into the city

rode two men. They were Sir Bedivere, King Arthur's long-time friend and close advisor; and Sir Kay, the King's brother—technically his foster brother, though neither of them ever felt anything but the closest of familial ties. In his initial act of kingship, Arthur had appointed Kay to be his seneschal.

It was these two men who, a few months earlier, had spirited the Queen away to the Tower of London in order to thwart Mordred's matrimonial intentions. Now they were back, though the Queen wasn't with them. In a city normally rife with rumors, there was a surprising lack of them concerning the Queen. Was she still in the Tower? Or had she gone elsewhere? No one knew—or seemed much to care.

Cheers rang out. The two knights paused in their riding to enjoy the moment. When they each raised an acknowledging hand, the cheers rang out even louder than before.

Simon stood before the door of the chandler's shop taking in the colorful scene. Although he didn't know the men, he found the people's euphoria contagious. For the first time, he felt that he, too, was truly a citizen of Uther Pendragon's magnificent city. He felt like he belonged. And so, without hesitation, Simon added his own cheering voice to all the others.

The two men were pleased by the enthusiastic welcome. They were delighted to be back in the city once more, and delighted to learn that Queen Margause had departed, along with her slimy retinue. And yet their feelings were muted by their lack of knowledge of the King, of his whereabouts and his well-being.

Soon they each took up their old quarters in the citadel. Immediately, they passed orders for the palace to be prepared for royal occupation. It would soon be occupied by someone. Whether that would be the King himself, or else his successor, they didn't know.

❖

The men had already carried the King down to the boat and settled him in as comfortably as possible. Lute, now up and about, stood holding the boat's painter, anticipating their departure. They waited for Nimuë, who was just now descending the path toward the little inlet. Sister Eloise was with her.

The two women paused, thirty yards away, to say their farewells. From within the fold of her habit Sister Eloise extracted a small leather pouch. She held it out to Nimuë, a knowing look on her face. Nimuë accepted it without speaking.

"I truly do not know the formula," Sister Eloise said.

"Nor do I," Nimuë replied.

"I read it once, a long time ago, but the names of a few of the plants that it mentioned have remained in my mind. So perhaps the items in the pouch will be of some help to you. Nimuë, I hope and pray that you will be able to save him."

"He's worth saving."

"All men are worth saving."

"Him more than most," Nimuë said.

"All of you will be in my prayers. Now, sister, God go with you." Sister Eloise leaned forward and kissed Nimuë on the cheek.

Nimuë smiled, then spun about and hurried toward the boat where the men awaited her.

Chapter 30

I *told* Arthur she wasn't wholesome for him. I *warned* him against marrying her," Merlyn said, though there was no one there to hear him. "I *told* him she was destined to love another."

"Yes," came a second voice from inside Merlyn's head, "but you didn't tell him he *mustn't* marry her. You told him that where a man's heart is, there shall it be."

"There's no one who knows the truth of that statement better than I," Merlyn replied to the inner voice.

"Sadly, that is so," replied the voice inside his head.

"It was *worth* it," Merlyn insisted. "Besides, my relationship with Nimuë was fated."

"Hah. You don't believe in fate. You believe in reaping what you sow. And you didn't even get from her what you wanted most."

"No, I didn't. But the game isn't over just yet. Who knows how it will come out in the end?"

"Not you, that's for sure."

❖

The boat glided smoothly into the broad estuary. The rays of the December sun, now low in the west, reflected off the high white walls and towers of the citadel in the city, just a few miles distant. It was a familiar sight to the knights and a welcome one.

It had been an easy sea voyage from Ynys Rhonech, the winds and waves fully cooperating. During the entire short sea journey, Nimuë had stood with one arm about the mast, humming softly. Was she singing to the water? Or was she crooning a hymn to the ailing King, who lay just a few feet from her? Whatever the case, it seemed to have the right effect, calming the waters and the King.

"You're nearly home, sire," Nimuë said softly. And for the first time, Arthur opened his eyes.

"Home?" the King said, in a croaky voice.

"Yes. We'll carry you to the city in the morning. Tonight, you must rest."

She lowered a dipper into a bucket of fresh water and put it to his mouth. He drank most of it greedily, spilling some of it on his neck and chest.

"Home," the King said wistfully. "You don't know how many times in the last two years I've dreamed of being home again."

"You're nearly there, sire. Tomorrow we shall make that dream a reality."

"Please excuse my ignorance," the King said, "but who might you be?"

"No one especially important, sire, though we share two close friends."

"Two close friends? And who might they be?"

"One of them is called Merlyn and the other Sir Pelleas."

"My word. And what are you called?" the King asked.

When the King opened his eyes the next morning, there was Sir Kay, just arrived from the city, grinning at him.

"Lord, brother," the King said, "what a frightful way in which to begin a new day. Couldn't you find it in your heart to allow me a more congenial method of awakening than having to look straight into *your* beastly countenance?"

"Welcome home, Arthur," Kay replied, ignoring the playful insult. Though not a medical man, even to Kay's untutored eye his brother looked to be in a perilous condition. It was no time for jokes. "I'm sorry to say that a rather modest and nondescript conveyance awaits you, sire. We thought it best to get you up the palace with as little fanfare as possible. You can greet the people more properly later, when you are more up to it."

"Yes. That would probably be best."

"We have summoned all the finest physicians, sire. They will be awaiting your arrival in the palace."

"Thank you, Kay. I will listen to them. But I have two very fine physicians already." He pointed at Lute and Nimuë, who were waiting close by. "I hope there is room for them in your nondescript conveyance."

"I'm sure there will be." Lute looked vaguely familiar to Sir Kay, but he had never seen the woman named

Nimuë. He wondered who she might be.

The small group moved slowly over the road that ran beside the estuary. Gradually the estuary narrowed, and then they moved up a more twisty road through the water meadows until they reached the bridge before the city gates. When they entered the city, a few of the people frequenting the lowest square became aware of them, but they didn't pay them much attention. None of them realized that the rather plain-looking coach now moving upward toward the citadel bore the King, his brother Sir Kay, and several of the most notable people in the land.

One person who did, however, was Tom. He and Simon were crossing the square when Tom noticed the party passing beneath the raised inner portcullis. He placed a hand on the boy's shoulder and said, "Simon, hold on just a moment, if ya wouldn't mind."

The boy looked nonplussed but did as Tom asked. He saw where Tom's eyes were directed. He, too, began to stare at the group.

"That feller in front on the lanky roan, that's Sir Craddock," Tom said. "And the feller seated up beside the coach driver, that's Sir Sagramour. Inside the coach, can ya see the heads of several people?"

"Yes, I can see 'em."

"Ya see anyone in there ya might recognize?"

The boy squinted and looked hard as he could. "Tom," he suddenly cried, "I *recognize* one of 'em. Whatta ya know 'bout that, Tom? One of 'em's the Earl of Sanham. One of 'em's Lute!"

❖

The King's return soon became known throughout the city. But the fact that he made no public appearances was dismaying. When it became common knowledge that he'd been seriously injured, daily prayers were said for him in the minster, and many other prayers were said privately throughout the city. The Feast of the Nativity came and went, and with it, hopes for the King began to dwindle.

In the palace, Arthur alternated between short but lucid periods of consciousness and longer spells of total unconsciousness. The King's physicians remained optimistic. Nimuë, however, felt otherwise. The one hope she maintained was that she would be able to unlock the mysteries of the Three Marys' Ointment. She felt sure that she possessed most of what she needed; but she knew neither the manner of preparation nor the desired proportions. Every night she experimented, and a couple of times she thought she might actually have achieved it. But when she surreptitiously rubbed some of it on Arthur's brow, only a momentary improvement occurred. Yes, she thought, it must be true—that ointment was created only one time and for just one purpose, the holiest of purposes. This wasn't it. Well, it had been worth trying for it.

Chapter 31

On the 27th of December, St. John's Day, King Arthur awoke to a bright and chilly morning. For once he felt like he was in his right senses, so he immediately sent messengers to summon Sir Kay, Sir Bedivere, Sir Craddock, Sir Sagramour, and Lute to his royal apartments in the palace.

Tom had come to see Lute and was with him in his small chamber when the messenger brought Lute the message that he'd been summoned by the King. After the man's departure, Tom couldn't help noticing how somber Lute's mood had suddenly become. Being no fool, Tom quickly realized what the topic of conversation amongst the highest nobles was likely to be.

He didn't envy Lute. He knew his long-time friend was about to face an agonizing decision. He suspected that Lute, given his druthers, would never accept the kingship. But what if Lute felt he had little choice? Tom suspected that Lute, in such a case, would set his own desires aside and do what duty and honor required.

When Lute and the other knights entered the King Arthur's apartments, they found the King propped up in his bed, swathed in a heavy layer of warm bedclothes. Two of his physicians sat beside him, but when all the knights had gathered, he dismissed the physicians. This was going to be a most important private consultation.

"Sire," the men said, all of them dropping to one knee.

"Please," Arthur said, "come and sit close to me. I want you to be able to hear my voice, such as it is."

Kay sat down on the edge of the bed next to his brother. Lute sat farthest away, across the room on a three-legged chair draped with animal pelts.

"Lute, won't you pull your chair up closer to me, my son?"

The other knights took careful note of the king's last phrase. Did he mean it as a casual endearment? Or did he mean it literally?

"My physicians have done all they can," he said. "To their credit, they haven't given up hope. But they are foolish optimists. The game is nearly over."

"Oh no, brother!" Kay exclaimed. "You mustn't think that."

"Nimuë has proved herself the best of my physicians. She has helped alleviate my pain far more than the others. But even she can't fend off the inevitable. No, my dear friends, we must now accept that. And now, most importantly, we must consider the future of our people. We must decide who it is who will rule them, who it is who will be my successor. I need your help. I didn't do so well when I appointed Mordred the Prince Regent, did I? We've all suffered because of that foolishness. This time we must do better."

Silence filled the room. The knights looked at each other, waiting for someone to speak.

"It should be someone in the bloodline," Kay said, finally breaking the silence. "It must be someone who qualifies in that way, but it must also be a person with the right qualities of heart and mind."

"I can only think of one such person," the King said. He was now staring at Lute, who squirmed a bit in his seat. "And the person I am thinking of may take some persuading."

"And who would that be, sire?" asked Sir Bedivere. He glanced toward Lute, then back at Arthur.

Arthur's eyes remained on Lute. Lute returned his gaze unflinchingly.

"The man I have in mind is a high-ranking nobleman and a man who is in direct descent from my father's father. His name is—"

"Duke Constantine," said Sir Kay.

"Who?" said Sir Craddock. "Duke Constantine?"

"He's the son of Uther's younger brother, Cador. He's the Duke of Less Britain."

Arthur still stared at Lute. The others began to wonder why. Arthur, it seemed was waiting for a sign from Lute.

Then it came, as Lute slowly nodded his agreement. "He sounds like just the man," Lute said.

Then Arthur slowly, hesitantly, answered Lute's nod with one of his own.

"I quite like him," said Sir Sagramour. "In Brittany his

reputation is impeccable. And he gave us aid and comfort in our struggles against Launcelot. Duke Constantine is a most honorable man."

Sir Bedivere hadn't yet offered an opinion. He kept his eyes on Lute for a lengthy moment, then turned them toward the King. "Well," he said at last, "I was hoping for someone else. But I find no fault in your choice. Duke Constantine bears a most illustrious name."

"Indeed he does," said the King. "Let us hope he will live up to it."

Tom had remained in Lute's chamber, hoping to learn the results of this fateful meeting. He looked up as Lute re-entered the chamber. "Well, Sir Earl," he said, "should I be a-droppin' to one knee?"

Lute smiled wanly. "No, not now, and not ever. Tom, you and I are friends. *Equal* friends. You will never be my vassal."

"So . . . I reckon ya must've told 'em 'no', eh Lute?"

"Not in so many words."

"Does ya have any regrets?"

Lute, lost in thought for a moment, didn't reply. Finally he said, "You know, if it had been necessary, I would have agreed. But it turned out that it wasn't." To Tom, Lute's words seemed to be tinged with regret.

"Lute—and this ain't just friendship a-speakin'—you woulda made a wonderful king."

"Well . . . maybe . . . . But I guess that's something we will never know, will we."

Chapter 32

Lyonore was broadcasting grain to the small flock of hens she'd turned loose in her vegetable patch, a practice she usually followed during the winter months to help fertilize the soil for the springtime replanting. She looked up at the sudden sound of horse's hooves approaching on the lane that led to her small house. A solitary rider was approaching. It was her son.

Lute swung himself down off the horse somewhat awkwardly and raised a hand in greeting. He had to stoop a bit to share a hug with her, his mother being nearly a head shorter than he was.

"Lute, you're walking with a limp. You've been injured."

"Yes, but my thigh is on the mend. The wound itself has healed entirely, and finally the muscles have decided to begin working properly again. They had me worried there for a few days."

The woman stared into her son's face. She steeled herself in preparation for learning the reason for her son's unexpected visit. Lute, reading her thoughts, didn't hesitate to deliver his message.

"Mother, he wants to see you," he said.

"He?" she replied in a barely audible voice.

Lute nodded. "Yes. The King."

Lyonore gazed off into the distance. It was several seconds before she returned her eyes to her son's face. "How is he?" she asked.

"He's dying. It may already be too late. But, if you're willing, we can try to get there in time. It will take us three or four days, and he may not last that long."

She hardly hesitated before saying, "Of course, Lute. If he wishes it, and if you wish it, then we must try."

"Do *you* wish it, mother?"

She slowly nodded, her lips compressed. "For many years I wished it. Then I gave up hoping for it."

"Can we leave first thing in the morning?"

"Of course. But tonight, you must rest. I will need to gather a few things and then I'll be ready."

"Rob and Matthew will be going with us. Rob can lend you a gentle mount."

"No need, Lute. I have more horses than just the old gelding who once served you so well."

Lute smiled. "You still have him? Then I must go and say hello. I have really missed the old fellow."

"Yes, he's very old. But I'm sure he hasn't forgotten you."

"He was very old ten years ago." Lyonore smiled. "He and Matthew have become quite good friends," she said. "I think he thinks Matthew is you. Matt is very much like you were at that age."

"Then I'll likely confuse the old fellow thoroughly."

"He'll be as glad to see you as I am," Lyonore said.

❖

It was four days later that Yonec led Lute and Lyonore up the set of steps that led to the walkway atop the curtain wall, the walkway that linked the citadel to the palace. They both hesitated for a moment and stared down it. It evoked very different recollections for each of them.

For Lyonore, the sight took her back nearly thirty years to the half a dozen times she had crossed it. Each day that week, Merlyn had led her along the walkway to the palace and then taken her to a small chamber where she had her private rendezvous with Arthur. At that time the two of them had still been just teenagers. Each successive day, the pair of young people had gradually come to know each other, their comfort and affection growing to the point where she and Arthur had begun to fall in love. On Lyonore's final visit, they had consummated that love. Now, as she stepped across this oft-remembered space, she felt more trepidatious than she could remember feeling during the intervening years.

Lute's memories of the walkway were far more recent. They were of a night about three months ago, when he and Neely, following Tom's directions, had crept out onto the dark walkway, seeking a particular tree by which they might descend to the garden below and make their escape from the citadel. Lute smiled, remembering his easy descent of the tree, followed by Neely's misadventure when the branch he'd grasped snapped off, sending him plunging down through all the lower branches and landing hard on the grassy space below. Neely had been terrified, but his fall had caused him no serious harm. A few minutes later, the two of them completed their escape, baffling the guards who'd been perplexed by the sounds made by Neely's fall.

When Lyonore and Lute reached the entry to the palace, Yonec greeted the sentries outside the main door to the palace. They nodded at him familiarly and opened the door. A broad set of steps ascended from the resplendent entryway up to the royal chambers. The three of them climbed up to a wide gallery off of which there were several doors both to the left and the right. Yonec let them to the right to a doorway flanked by a pair of guards. Just as they arrived there, the door came open and two men and a woman stepped through. The men, who were the King's physicians, nodded to the threesome. The woman, Nimuë, smiled at Lute and said, "He's awake and seems to be feeling fairly well at the moment. He knows you're here."

"Nimuë, this is my mother," Lute said.

"Yes, I'd guessed as much. Madam, it's an honor to meet you."

Lyonore was somewhat taken aback by this confident and strikingly attractive young woman. Who was she? she wondered. Could she actually be one of the King's physicians? Lute seemed to know her, at any rate.

"I shall wait for you out here," Yonec said. "Stay with

the King as long as you need to."

"No more than a few minutes, please," said Nimuë. "He tires quickly."

"No, we won't stay long," Lyonore's replied. "Thank you," she said to Yonec, who dipped his head in acknowledgment.

Yonec held the door open, for them, and Lyonore and Lute stepped through.

Chapter 33

At the sound of the footsteps, Arthur looked up. There before him stood Lyonore. It had been nearly thirty years since he had last seen her, but he recognized her immediately. He smiled, and she returned his smile with a shy smile of her own.

"Lyonore, you've come," he said in a raspy voice she could barely hear.

"Yes, sire, I have," she replied, her voice sounding just slightly deeper than he remembered.

To her, the King was recognizable, though he was but a shadow of the robust youth he'd once been—his cheeks were pale and hollow, his once shiny light-brown hair now lank and lusterless, his neck so terribly thin. And yet he was still the man about whom she held long-cherished memories, the man who had caused her the greatest joys and greatest sorrows of her life.

"Come and sit," he said, patting the edge of his bed. "I want so much to have you near to me. Lyonore, it means a great deal to me that you've come."

"And to me, my lord, to be with you once again."

❖

When Lyonore entered the chamber two days later on her second visit to the King, she was accompanied by a young boy. The boy took two steps toward the King's bed and dropped to one knee. He dipped his head forward respectfully.

"He wanted very much to meet his grandfather," Lyonore said. "I hope you don't mind that I brought him. His name is Matthew. He's Lute's son."

Tears formed in the King's eyes. It required an effort, but he raised his right hand and placed it on the kneeling boy's head. The King seemed more feeble to Lyonore than on her previous visit.

"Matthew," he said in just more than a whisper, "it gives me joy to meet you. I wish I had known you longer."

"Sire," the boy said, "the picture of you I carved on my mother's tray isn't as handsome as you truly are. But it does look a bit like you."

"Picture of me?" Arthur said. "You carved my likeness? How could you do that, never having seen me?"

"Oh, sire, from my grandmother's painting of you."

Arthur looked at Lyonore for an explanation. The woman looked embarrassed.

"I showed Matthew a painting I once made of you, shortly after Lute was born."

"Why did you paint such a picture?" he asked. Again she looked embarrassed.

"I didn't want to forget what you looked like."

"And did that ever happen?"

"Actually, it never did."

❖

Lute and Matthew stood just outside the door to the large room where the fencers were hard at it. For Lute, the place brought back many memories, most of them good ones. But he couldn't help thinking about the young men with whom he'd trained, young men who'd become his friends, some of whom had become illustrious knights—most of them now dead.

"Lute? I thought I recognized you." The speaker was Sir Ascomour, the fencing master.

"Hello, sir," Lute replied. "I'm surprised you remember me."

"Nonsense, Lute, how could I forget one of my finest pupils?"

"Sir, this is my son, Matthew. Matthew, this is Sir Ascomour, who patiently guided me through the fundamentals of fencing."

"He learned quickly, Matthew, as I bet you will, too, in a few years when you come to us for your training."

"Oh, father, can I?"

"If it's what you want."

"I'm sure it will be."

"Matthew," said Sir Ascomour, reaching out to shake the boy's hand, "I shall look forward to teaching you. It will be a real pleasure to have someone like Lute here again."

❖

Mary's father, the chandler, had agreed to allow Simon to go each afternoon to the minster and join with the young novices in their classes there. Father Urias was delighted to have Simon, a little chap with extraordinary intellectual curiosity, back. He saw in Simon great scholarly potential, potential he wished some of the other boys might possess.

It was as Simon had begun to make his way back down from the city's second level that the boy heard someone shouting his name—"Simon! Hey, Simon!"

It was Matthew. The two boys ran to meet each other, then clasped each other by the shoulders.

"Grandmother," Matthew announced, "this is my friend, Simon."

"The one whose likeness you put on the tray? Yes, I can see that."

Simon didn't know what she was talking about, but he didn't care, he was so delighted to see his friend. "So you've come from Sanham?" Simon asked.

"Well . . . yes, I suppose you could say that. Oh, Simon, this is my grandmother. She's my father's mother."

"Your ladyship," Simon said respectfully, whipping off his cap and holding it in front of him, "it's an honor."

"It is for me, too, Simon. Matthew speaks of you often."

"Listen, Matt, I know all about making candles and tapers and rush lights. Want to see? Come with me and I'll show you."

"Those are good things to know about, Simon," said Lyonore. "Will you show me as well?"

"With pleasure, your ladyship," the boy said. "C'mon, then, it's not far at all."

Chapter 34

In the city's great minster on the Eve of St. Hilary's Day, January 13th, they held the funeral mass for the King. The nave of the great edifice was filled with the city's sad and sober citizens. The procession of knights and nobles wasn't nearly as extensive or spectacular as usual, since so many of them hadn't returned from the recent fateful events, but a few dukes, earls, and knights, along with their ladies, were present.

Earl Thomas and Julianna processed slowly down the central aisle. Behind them walked a woman with a boy on each side of her—Lyonore, with Matthew and Simon each holding one of her hands. A pair of tall, broad-shouldered men followed the threesome, one of them the young Earl of Sanham. No one knew who the other man was, though he wore the clothing of a commoner. He was Rob, Lute's boyhood friend. When they had reached the front of the nave, the entire group moved to the earl's regular seats far to the left on the row closest to the chancel arch.

Tom and Mary and Magdalene, as was their wont, had come early and taken seats on a stone bench in the back corner of the north porch, a spot from which they had a good view of the event.

A few of the King's most venerable knights were present—men such as Sir Ascomour, the fencing master, and Sir Mador de la Porte, the riding master, men who had remained behind when the King and so many of his knights had gone across the water to confront Launcelot. The most illustrious figures present, however, were Sir Kay, the King's brother, Sir Bedivere, the King's close friend and advisor, and Sir Sagramour and Sir Craddock, two of the knights who'd survived the catastrophic battle with Mordred.

It was a solemn service. The dark-robed monks, standing in rows in their choir stalls, intoned several of the penitential psalms, ending with King David's plaintive cry: "Thou shalt wash me, and I shall be made whiter than snow." The bishop offered a lengthy mediation, with special emphasis on the verse from the 23rd Psalm, "thy rod and thy staff, they comfort me."

He ended his mediation with a reading from *Ecclesiasticus*: "Let us now praise famous men . . . Some of these men have gained glory and were praised in their days; and some have left no memorial; they have perished as if they had never been. But these were men of mercy, and good things continue with their seed; their seed shall not be forgotten; let the people show forth their wisdom and the Church declare their praise. Their bodies are buried in peace, but their names liveth unto generation and generation."

At the service's conclusion, the bishop led the entire congregation in reciting the Pater Noster, the Lord's Prayer. Then the citizens of the city waited and watched as the nobles processed out of the minster, back out into the bitingly cold air of the mid-January day.

At the home of Earl Thomas, Rob and Lyonore prepared to leave for Northering. Lute and Matthew would not be going with them but would be going home to Sanham. Lute had been away since that October day, three months earlier, when Colgrevaunce and his men had come for him. Matthew, who'd been whisked away to safety in Northering, had been away for more than two months, and Simon had been gone for roughly the same amount of time.

After seeing his mother and his friend off at the city gates, Lute, along with Matthew, went to the chandler's shop to collect Simon and Tom. Tom planned to go along with them to Sanham and then bring Simon back to the city. Simon longed to go home to see his grandfather, but he was also adamant in his desire to continue studying with Father Urias; he hoped his grandfather would agree to it. He longed, more than anything, to learn about books.

As Tom was saying his farewells to Mary, Mary's friend, the woman named Magdalene, shyly approached Lute.

"Sir," she said, "please pardon me for asking ya, but the tall quiet fellow who was up there in the little chamber with you and the lad, he's one of your men in Sanham?"

"Yes, he is. He's one of the very best," Lute replied.

She nodded.

"During those days when the three of yas was all locked up in the citadel," she said, "I suppose he musta been missing his wife and children."

"No, I don't think so," Lute replied, "since he has no wife and children.'

"Goodness sakes, why not? A fine strappin' fellow like him."

"When it comes to women, Brogan's always been a bit fussy. I rather think he's been holding out for someone special."

"Well, a fine fella like he is, it would make no sense if he was willin' ta settle for anything less than the best."

"Ha, ha, ha, I quite agree. How would you like to come along with us and tell him that?"

Magdalene, her hand cradling her chin, looked thoughtful. "Sir do you mean it? Do you really think it would be all right if I did?"

"Absolutely," Lute said. "come along with us."

"Well," she said, "perhaps I shall."

CHAPTER 35

The January sun had dipped behind the treetops when Willykin and Eldred, standing guard at the gate to the manor house, saw the small clutch of riders approaching. One of the first riders, they realized almost immediately, was Lute, the Earl of Sanham. Beside him rode a woman they didn't recognize. Behind the first pair came three smaller figures, one riding atop the pony named Swifty and one riding on a smallish horse. They were Matthew and Simon, for sure. The third rider was a little man whose name, they knew from previous events, was Tom.

"Sir!" shouted Willykin, "welcome home, sir!" Eldred remained silent, but as the earl passed by, he tugged at his forelock.

"Matthew, welcome home, laddy!" Willykin shouted again. "And Simon, welcome to you, boyo! How glad I am to see the both of yas, safe and sound. We was plenty worried 'bout yas. And Tom, ya be most welcome, too. Ya come ta stay?"

"Ah, no, 'fraid not. I just come along to keep Lute and the boys company. I'll be a-takin' that there lad"—he pointed to Simon—"back to the city after he's had hisself a good visit with his grandfather. That young lad's decided he wants ta be a city feller. Smart lad, that Simon."

"And what about you, Tom? What're you a-plannin' ta do?"

"Me? Oh, I reckon I'm a-plannin' on makin' candles and makin' babies, not necessarily in that order."

"Ha, ha. Good on you, Tom."

Standing high up on the roof of the barn close to the edge was a tall man with a hammer in his hand. He looked down at the little group of riders, and as he did, the woman riding beside Lute glanced up and saw him. So did Lute.

"Brogan!" Lute shouted. "I certainly hope to Goodness you haven't gone and finished up that job I left undone up there a few months back. I've been looking forward to getting back to it again."

"Well, it's too late, sir. You got here just five minutes too late."

The woman on the horse next to Lute hadn't escaped Brogan's notice. "Sir, that woman you got there a-ridin' along beside you—could she is be someone I've seen before?"

"I believe she might be. She decided she wanted to come along with us, Brogan. Seems she has something she wants to say to you."

"Why, what a coincidence, sir. I have something I'd like to say to her."

"Well, all in good time, Brogan. Now, you be careful climbing down from up there."

"Oh, sir, don't you go confusin' me with Neely, sir. I've

a far better head for heights than that lad does." Brogan burst into laughter at the thought of Neely being up there a-workin' on the barn's roof, just a-shakin' in his boots. Lute joined in his laughter.

Magdalene couldn't help smiling at the men's banter. She had known all along that she'd done the right thing, trying to help these men after Mordred had clapped them into that little set of rooms high up in the citadel. She wondered now if she would ever see the citadel again. She figured there was quite a good chance she never would, and that would be just fine with her.

On the covered gallery of the manor house, Jillian stood with her arm about Editha, the two of them watching as the little troupe of riders began crossing the manor forecourt.

When Lute saw his wife and daughter awaiting them, tears formed in his eyes. He raised an arm in greeting.

❖

Merlyn was taking sips from a mug of a spicy herb tea he'd just brewed. He'd made it from a recipe Nimuë had taught him. He stood near the front of his cave, looking out through the transparent but very real wall that sealed him inside this home of his, a home that was also a prison. He imagined the breeze brushing against his face, a breeze whose feel he was denied. His experiences of the real world were very muted now. He could still hear the birds and the sounds of the river, but he couldn't smell the flowers or feel the warmth of the sun—though now, in late January, the sun gave little warmth anyway.

The tea tasted sweet to his palate. It made him think of Nimuë. Well, best not to do that. He'd had enough sadness and disappointment in his life without doing that. And yet, he couldn't help it. What a joy it had been for him to have met her, to have come to know her, to have taught her, and to have desired her. That enigmatic young woman had enriched his life immeasurably, and in most unexpected ways. He couldn't find it in his heart to bear her any ill will. She was what she was. And what she was, he reflected, was truly remarkable.

The sun had passed its zenith now and was creating sparkles on the surface of the Wye—light dancing on water, one of the great natural beauties of the world.

Merlyn's reverie was interrupted by the whinnying of a horse. "Holy Jerusalem," Merlyn said out loud, "if that doesn't sound like Raguel."

Merlyn stared out through the transparent veil, and there in an open space across the river he could see the great black horse. The horse raised his head and whinnied again, almost as if in greeting. "Rags, you old rascal," Merlyn said, "you've come back."

"And he's not the only one," came a soft voice from just behind him. Merlyn whirled about. There stood the young woman he'd been meditating about.

"You?" he managed to stammer.

"Yes," she said, "me."

"Come to stay?"

"Well, we shall have to see."

❖ ❖ ❖